FATHOMS
A NOVEL OF THE PARANORMAL

LARRY L. DEIBERT

COVER ART BY SARA LORENZ

COVER PHOTO BY LARRY L. DEIBER

Peggy
Without your love and support, I would not have been able to write this book. Thanks for sharing your life with me. I love you.

ACKNOWLEDGMENTS

Thank you, Dr. Barry Slaven, for the assistance you gave with the medical questions I had.

Thanks, Linda Furlow-Patty, for your support and your corrections. This is the second time you edited one of my works and I look forward to your assistance in the near future.

Thank you, Nick Zumas. You always find the mistakes overlooked by those of us who have read and edited my books before you had the opportunity to read the manuscript.

Thank you to my daughter, Laura Deibert Beck. I have always appreciated the work you put into my book; the suggestions you offered and using your teacher's abilities to make my words a little better. I love you.

Thank you, Peggy Deets Deibert. Since I met you nearly twelve years ago, you have been my constant companion and soon we will be married nine years. Thanks for all the support you have given me and for usually being the final reader and editor before publication. I love you always.

Grantville, Pennsylvania
Emporia, Virginia

1

Brandon and JoAnne Pederson stepped outside the Hollywood Casino into the sweltering heat. Even as they waited for their car to be brought to them by the valet, the temperature, hovering around 95 degrees, didn't bother them at all. Both of them remained quiet until they hopped in their air-conditioned Hyundai Sonata and drove toward the highway. Looking over at his wife with a huge smile on his face, he tapped fists with her and exclaimed, "Wow, honey you really killed it in there! How much did you win, anyway?"

"1,117 dollars! You won too, didn't you?"

He looked in his rearview mirror and then pressed down on the accelerator to merge with the oncoming traffic, relatively light today. "I only won 238 dollars but I was down a hundred and seventy-five at one point. It scared the crap out of me that I was going to lose the money I had set aside for golf this week." He leaned on the horn when a driver nearly cut him off. "It was sure nice to be lucky for a change, wasn't it?"

She had the visor pulled down and was applying some lipstick and checking her hair, which she felt needed a little brushing. Yeah, it was, honey. Now we can really have a nice vacation. I can't wait to get there tomorrow. The place we rented sounds so cool."

"It sure does. It was built in 1899 and has been in the Wright family for a very long time. I am looking forward to meeting Steve and Mary and see what kind of people they are. Both sounded very pleasant on the phone."

He glanced over at her and saw her yawn and close her eyes. He knew she would probably sleep for several hours, so he turned up the Sirius radio and punched in the 60s channel. He loved that music because that's what was mainly listened to when he was growing up. He also loved classic country, Irish tunes and Christian rock.

2

Two and a half hours later, JoAnne stretched and opened her eyes. She threw Brandon a devilish smile and inquired, "Are we there yet, daddy?"

"I made pretty good time. We passed Martinsburg, Virginia about fifteen minutes ago. I think we should stop around Harrisonburg and get gas and a bite to eat. Then you can take the wheel until we stop for the night."

He saw her nod. "Sounds like a plan. Wake me when we get there."

He smiled and shook his head. The woman could sleep.

3

Brandon met JoAnne Saylor in October of '03 at a Cowboys/Eagles game in Philly.. She was a diehard Eagles fan and started giving him crap when he sat next to her. He was wearing a Cowboys jacket and cap and was one of the few fans of the Texas team seated in that section.

"You sure you're sitting in the right seat? This is Eagles country not Cowgirls."

He saw her smile as she taunted him and he figured he'd give it back to her. "Cooked Eagle is going to be a great dinner, tonight, miss."

"JoAnne Saylor. You wanna put a little money where your mouth is, cowboy?"

"Yes, ma'am. How about after the game, loser buys dinner? I'm Brandon Pedersen from Wilkes Barre."

"Okay, Brandon from WB, you are on"

Brandon went nuts when the Cowboys drew first blood, but the Eagles tied the game in the second quarter.

'Da Boys' scored twice taking a ten point lead and the trash talk was nonstop. When the Eagles took a one point lead with less than five minutes to go, Eagles fans were on their feet and JoAnne had the chance to get her licks in.

With a little over a minute left, his Cowboys won the game on a Billy Cundiff field goal.

4

After the game they met at Marra's on Passyunk Avenue where they enjoyed pizza, beer and lively conversation. She was an interior designer in Reading, and she was also taking online courses, working toward a BS in that field. She had grown up in a home with zealous Philadelphia Eagles fans and they tried to talk her into trying out for the cheerleader squad, but prancing around in scanty clothes was not her style.

"So what do you do, Brandon from WB?" She inquired before throwing down the last of her glass of beer and then chewing a mouthful of pizza.

"I'm a nurse at the VA clinic.. My grandfather was in the Navy during World War II and he served on the battleship North Carolina." Brandon took a sip of his beer. "It is so rewarding to assist in caregiving for the brave men and women who require our services. I have heard many stories from them and I've been keeping a journal. Someday I might even write a book."

"I never had any family that served in the military. Is your grandfather still alive?"

After he swallowed the pizza he was chewing and wiped his mouth with his napkin, he answered, "No he went missing on his battleship. I guess he fell overboard because he was never found.

"That's so sad. Is your grandmother still alive?"

"Yeah Grandma Eleanor's still with us and pretty feisty at eighty-two. When we kids were little and we'd do something that upset her she'd call us little shits. I love that woman dearly and someday I want to go to North Carolina and visit my grandpa's ship. It's a museum on the Cape Fear River in Wilmington."

JoAnne listened intently. When he mentioned the ship, a strange look came over his face and she was momentarily troubled but the feeling passed and she just ignored the emotion.

Something coursed through his body. It almost felt as though he had stuck his finger in an electrical socket. The sensation only lasted for a few seconds but he saw that she had noticed. That too only lasted for a moment and then she smiled at him as though nothing at all happened, but her eyes betrayed her. He was certain she felt afraid of him, and it disturbed him.

After finishing their meals, they walked to her car, which was closest; his was a couple of blocks away. Darkness had fallen while they were eating, and there was a chill in the early evening air. He put an arm around her to keep her warm and she leaned in toward him.

A couple of Eagles fans were passing by and when they saw his jacket and cap, one of them said, "Fuck you, Cowboy. You got so lucky. Next time we'll kick your asses." The guy elbowed him and laughed as he and his buddy walked away.

"Man, some of the fans in this town really suck, JoAnne. It's only a game, yet you'd think that when the Eagles, and probably even the Phillies, lose, the losses are going to be life changing. A co-worker took his son and son-in-law to a Phillies game when they were playing his favorite team, the Cardinals. His son is a Phillies fan and his son-in-law roots for the Cubs. Anyway, the Redbirds won and while he was waiting for the boys to come out from the restroom, a pretty big, burly guy stopped in front of him, looked at his Cardinals t-shirt and cap and said, 'Fuck you and your Cardinals'. " He shrugged, "That's Philly for you."

When they arrived at JoAnne's car, even before he had

the chance to ask for it, she wrote her phone number on her business card.

"Brandon, I really had a great time and I want to see you again." She touched his face and smiled.

"Yeah, I want to see you too. I can come down to Reading after work on Friday and we could grab a meal or catch a movie…"

"Or, after that long drive, you could come to my place for dinner and we could watch TV and we'll see about finding you a place to stay."

"Cool, we could spend the weekend together. I've never been to Reading and you could show me around." He kissed her and then she hopped in her car and took off, waving her hand from the open window.

Eleven months later they married.

5

He pulled in to the Country Inn and Suites in Emporia, Virginia where they would spend the night.

When he awakened early the next morning, he drank a cup of coffee and stepped in the shower. Steam filled the bathroom and when he wiped off the mirror to shave, he saw a ghostly figure standing behind him. He dropped his razor and grabbed on to the counter with both hands to keep himself from falling. His breath was taken away and although he was not afraid, he had the feeling that this would not be the last specter he would ever see.

Quietly he dressed and exited the room heading for the hot breakfast offered by the hotel. The scents of coffee, eggs, sausage and potatoes wafted through the breakfast room. An eighty something lady was having a little trouble trying to extract her waffle from the waffle maker so he offered his help to which she nodded her head.

"Thank you so much young man. My arthritis acts up sometimes and it becomes difficult to do even the most menial tasks."

As he placed the waffle on her plate he inquired, "Are you here alone, ma'am?"

She shook her head. "No, my husband still hasn't come down. It takes him a little bit longer in the morning these days. He has some service connected disabilities from the fighting in Korea but he refuses to let me help him: he's becoming a stubborn old fool." The twinkle in her eyes showed him that she loved her husband dearly.

"If you need any help with anything else, please don't hesitate to ask. My wife likes to sleep in so I'll probably be in here for a good long time before I go back to the room to get her up."

The woman nodded and took her plate to a table where a couple her age was sitting.

Brandon studied the people beginning to fill the breakfast room. Two families with small kids took up two tables, pushing them together; the moms stayed with the kids while the dads started filling plates with food. One of the children, a boy about eight or nine was staring Brandon down, causing him to avert his eyes to another part of the room. A businessman in a suit sat down next to him, talking quite loudly on his Bluetooth as he placed his iPad on the table and began working earnestly on something. A woman in a business suit carrying two steaming cups of coffee came to the table, setting them down and then returned to the breakfast bar, loading up two plates. Three men with large bellies, wearing Vietnam Veteran and Proud caps sat down and focused on the television that was currently showing the weather.

After finishing his breakfast and grabbing another cup of coffee, he strolled outside for some fresh air. When he stepped through the doorway, two men and a woman were smoking and they blew smoke in his direction. He coughed and sneered at the trio. "Can't you all find somewhere else to smoke instead of right beside the door? Cigarette smoke really stinks. I have never had one and I never will! He stormed back inside leaving the smokers to finish their filthy habit.

He sat down on the sofa, still coughing. His cigarette allergy was getting worse but he needed to chill a little and let smokers enjoy the little space they had left. Smoking was banned in so many places and even though those people were making poor choices, he should not have been so rude. He momentarily entertained the thought of going out and apologizing, but it probably wouldn't have done any good; he just had to get better at this.

6

JoAnne awakened to a very chilly room. Nude, she briskly strolled to the air conditioner and turned it off. She didn't want to freeze when she hopped out of the tub. After the water temperature was 'just this side of scalding,' as Brandon put it, she stepped over the rim of the tub and closed the shower curtain. She spent a lot of time washing her hair, and then soaped herself all over before rinsing off. She opened the curtain and screamed. Brandon was standing there; he had not called out that he was back in the room and when JoAnne got startled, she couldn't stop herself from crying out loudly.

"Damn it, Brandon. You know I hate when you do that and you still try to scare the shit out of me." As he helped her out of the tub she continued, "One of these days you're going to scare me to death." She looked in his eyes. "Then it won't be so fucking funny, will it."

He lowered his head sheepishly. "I'm sorry, honey, but you are so easy and I doubt if you'll ever be scared to death. I'll try to start to behave." He began to towel her off hoping to soothe her a little bit, and maybe even get lucky before they got back on the road again. They were both too tired for sex last night.

She saw his look in the mirror and shook her head. "Don't even think about it, mister. I want to get down to Wrightsville and get on that beach before the weather turns. Showers are coming in later today or early evening, and if we leave in less than a half an hour we should arrive around noon."

He slapped her butt. "Okay, let's get this show on the road, then; but tonight…." He returned to the bedroom and started gathering everything together.

She helped him finish packing and then quickly picked everything up and stepped out from the room. As soon as she did, she felt so much better. She looked toward Brandon and he seemed fine, so she assumed that he did not have any kind of paranormal experience in there.

They went to the counter and checked out, and were on the road at nine. JoAnne estimated that they would arrive at Wrightsville Beach by twelve-thirty.

Wednesday, June 18th, 2014

Wrightsville Beach

1

Brandon pulled the car into the parking lot in front of the Carolina Temple Island Inn at twelve thirty-five. The building appeared freshly painted and the porch already looked inviting. They got out of the car and walked up the stairs to the front of the three-sided porch. There were rocking chairs, white wicker chairs and a small wicker sofa in the front. Rockers and wicker chairs filled the side porch along with a chaise lounge. A hammock was strung up near the rear of the porch. He assumed the upstairs porch would be decorated in a similar manner.

After they walked through the front door, Steve Wright, the owner, was coming in through the back door. He was a happy-go-lucky looking guy with a thick body and legs. He wore a nice white beard and hair, reminiscent of that jolly old Christmas elf. Brandon wondered if he did some wrestling back in the day; he figured he'd probably find out later. Steve had a friendly smile and a thick Southern accent.

Once introductions were completed Steve asked, "Did you two have a nice drive down from Wilkes Barre?"

"We did," Brandon replied. "We were going to drive it in one day but decided to leave yesterday morning, stay overnight and have a short drive today. JoAnne is glad we did it that way because she is anxious to get to the beach. Any chance our room is ready?"

"Hang on and I'll check." He tapped his iPhone and asked his cleaning crew, then put the phone in his pocket. Nodding his head he said, "It's all ready for you. The keys are on the table. We'll settle up the bill before you guys leave on Sunday."

"Thanks, Steve. We appreciate that."

"You're welcome. Mary will be over later and we'll probably hang out on the back porch with whoever might be there. Every room is full, so we could have a pretty good gathering tonight. Have a great day." He walked through the front door.

While JoAnne went up to check out the room, Brandon walked out to the car to start get the suitcases, water, beer and soda. He suggested they go shopping later to get meats and cheeses for sandwiches and some snacks. They planned to eat out quite a bit, but one or two days it would be nice eating here.

When everything was put away, they both changed into their swimming suits; JoAnne was wearing Brandon's favorite bikini and when he saw her come out of the bathroom he smiled. "Honey, you are going to be the best looking woman on the beach."

She threw her arms him and gave him a kiss. "Thanks, Brandon from Wilkes Barre. You're not too shabby yourself." She squeezed his butt and ran out the room, with him in hot pursuit.

2

JoAnne opened the back door and saw a young couple sitting on two wicker chairs. She and Brandon nodded at them and then headed across the street to the beach.

He set the beach bag on the sand as she opened the chairs. They covered all exposed areas with sunscreen and then ran down into the water. Though it was pretty cold, they swam out about thirty yards and then bobbed around as waves kept crashing into them. After about five minutes of getting hammered with water, he was the first one to call it quits and swam back to shore. He looked back and screamed. He saw a submarine lift from under the waves about a hundred yards behind JoAnne.

Get out, JoAnne before that sub draws you in to its wake!" He shouted.

She heard him and turned around; there was nothing there and she got really scared. He believed in ghosts and she let him tell her of the things he had seen growing up, but now, claiming there was a submarine behind her with dozens of people standing up on the beach listening to him and looking out toward her was extremely upsetting. She swam to shore and fell into his arms. She whispered, "Honey, you have to stop doing things like this. There is no submarine out there and a lot of these people are beginning to laugh at you. I don't know why you thought you saw a sub, but I don't want you to wind up in a psych ward down here."

He settled down and nodded his head. "JoAnne, I wish I knew what was going on in my head 'cause it scares me a little too. I really did see a sub and it had a number on the conning tower, U-352. I feel fine now, but maybe when we go home, I'll have the VA docs check me out."

3

Later, they drove across the drawbridge and turned into the shopping complex where Harris Teeter was located. They needed groceries and after the events of today, JoAnne really needed some wine. After they came back from the beach, they showered together, made love and then rested awhile. It had been a long day so far: Brandon was adamant about seeing the sub and he just wouldn't let it go. She was trying to understand why these things were happening to him, but it was difficult.

4

The unusual occurrences began again several weeks ago at his grandmother's house in Kingston. She wanted them to bring things down from the attic for her to go through. She was determined that some of her things had to go.

JoAnne watched him as he rooted though the

memorabilia, bringing smiles to his face. He told stories about a few of the items and pictures he found. When he lifted a yellowing canvas duffle bag, she saw him tremble and he quickly put it back down on the floor.

"What's wrong? You look like somebody just stepped on your grave?" As soon as she said that his eyes grew large and his face perceptibly changed into someone she didn't know. It only lasted a moment but it really frightened her.

He saw her fear and quickly replied. "I haven't heard that phrase in a long time. I guess you must have heard it somewhere as well."

"Yeah, I remember my folks saying it occasionally. I guess it's been a part of our language for a long time." She felt that his mood changed back to the man she fell in love with and she just shrugged it off.

"This is my grandfather's sea bag. It was sent back to us by the Navy after his disappearance and it's always been locked. One time I was up here when I was a kid and saw it. I asked Gamma about it but she just told me to let it be. It was none of my business what was in there. I wonder if she has softened over the years and would allow me to open it in her presence." When Brandon first began to talk, he couldn't say grandma, it came out gamma and the name stuck.

"Only one way to find out. Let's go."

Brandon carried it down to the living room and set it on the floor.

She was sleeping, so he gently shook her awake. When her eyes opened she smiled and then she saw the bag, with Al's name and service number stenciled on the side, on the floor. "Why did you bring that down, Brandon? I told you years ago that what is inside is none of your business." She shook a finger at him.

"Gamma, don't you think it's time to open this bag.. JoAnne and I are going to visit the battleship in a few weeks and I'd like to know something about him before I see the last place he was alive."

She closed her eyes and sighed. "I have never opened that sea bag, so perhaps it is time for all of us to see what your grandpa saved." She reached into the drawer in the end table and pulled out a key and then she handed it to Brandon.

5

Brandon opened the door and stepped on the porch. He saw a reflection of the setting sun through a window of a house across the street. It had been a long day and thankfully he was feeling better. He knew he saw that submarine and that he wasn't crazy, but he wasn't sure if JoAnne believed him. Later, when she was asleep he thought he would Google that sub and see if it ever was off the North Carolina coast.

Two couples were already seated.

He introduced himself. "Hi. I'm Brandon Pederson. My wife, JoAnne will be out shortly."

One man stood up and shook his hand. "I'm Chuck Hilbert and this is my wife, Amy." He pointed to her and she said, "Hi Brandon. Nice to meet you."

The other man stood up and said, "I'm Rich Nash and my wife is Sara."

Brandon sat down just as JoAnne came out with two cans of Yuengling lager. She gave one to her husband and sat down beside him on the love seat. Introductions were once again made and the three couples settled in.

"So where are you folks all from?" JoAnne inquired.

"Rich and I are from Buford, South Carolina. Chuck and Amy are from Holland, Michigan. The four of us have been coming here the same week for three years. We just love this place and we adore Steve and Mary."

"We haven't met Mary yet, but Steve seems like a pretty nice guy. He looks like Santa Claus." JoAnne took a sip of her beer and looked toward Brandon who was staring off into space again. She wondered what was going through his mind.

"So where are you folks from?" asked Amy.

Brandon had snapped out of his reverie and replied. "We live in Wilkes Barre, Pennsylvania. I was born there and JoAnne moved there after she got her degree in interior decorating."

"Interior decorating is so cool, Jo." Sara said.

"Yeah, it is. I have been pretty lucky and I work for a great company. I've been doing it for about fifteen years and hope to have my own business in the near future."

"How about you, Brandon? What fills your days?" Rich inquired.

"I'm a nurse at the VA clinic."

Steve and Mary had just stepped on to the porch from the street. "VA clinic, huh. I know a lot of guys who receive treatment at the clinic in Wilmington. You guys and gals do great things for our veterans." He said, as they sat down on the swing. "You a vet, Brandon?"

"No, I'm not, but my dad and an uncle served in Vietnam. Uncle Al was in the navy, like my grandfather, and dad was an infantryman."

Mary asked, "Are they both okay?"

"Dad was handling his problems really well, but two years ago, he dropped dead from a heart attack that nobody saw coming. Al drinks a little too much, but he's doing well. Dad's death shook him up for awhile and he quit drinking, but he started up again. JoAnne's dad was awarded a Distinguished Service Cross." He looked toward her

She nodded and said, "Dad was in heavy combat and he once covered a Viet Cong grenade with his body, trying to save the lives of three of his friends. Fortunately, the grenade was a dud and dad didn't have to forfeit his life. Unfortunately, the near death experience bothered him for a long time and he committed suicide when I was three." Tears started rolling down her cheeks, but she continued.

"It took me a long time to accept that it is extremely difficult for someone to carry that kind of a burden. Not having him around to see me grow up really hurt for a long time. Excuse me, please." She stood up and walked back inside.

If silence could be deafening, that would be the best way to describe the following few moments. To Brandon, it even seemed as though the air itself was stilled. The other couples wanted to reach out to her, but he was pretty sure they would respect the time she might need. He had never seen her like that, although she told that story to quite a few people. He looked out to the street and saw a man wearing an army uniform stop and look up on the porch. He nodded and was gone before anyone else saw him.

Brandon went back up to the room to offer comfort to his wife.

6

He walked into the small comfortable room and saw her sitting on the bed. He sat down beside her and put an arm around her shoulder. After he kissed her cheek, he asked, "You okay?"

She nodded. "Actually I never felt better. I somehow feel as though a great weight has been lifted from me. That's about the best way I can explain it." She gazed into his eyes.

"Well, after you left, I looked out to the street and I'm pretty sure I saw your dad. He looked just like his picture. He nodded and then he was gone."

Her mouth opened, but she couldn't speak.

7

Just before Brandon went upstairs, Steve was watching him closely and saw him turn toward the street for a moment. Out of the corner of his eye, he saw a soldier dressed in jungle fatigues. The man nodded, smiled and then disappeared. Steve was not spooked because he had seen ghosts before. He was intrigued by his new guests and figured he'd better talk to them pretty soon.

"Steve, Steve, come back to planet earth," Mary chuckled.

"Oh, sorry, Mar. I was preoccupied for a moment. Have any of you guys seen or heard anything odd today?"

Rich and Sara nodded.

"Today on the beach, Brandon was screaming at JoAnne. She was in the ocean about thirty or forty yards out and he was yelling at her to be careful of the submarine about one hundred yards out. He said she was going to get sucked into its wake. I didn't want to say anything to anyone, and I'm sure quite a few people heard him. Is there something wrong with him?"

"I don't know, Rich, but maybe we should keep this a porch secret. Like the sign says 'What happens on the porch stays on the porch." He laughed. "I'll talk to him if he comes back out. If not I'll catch him tomorrow."

Steve sat quietly for several moments. He and several of his guests over the years had also seen the U352 rise up out of the ocean.

8

"Do you want to go out?"

"No. I think I'd like you to hold me awhile and then I'm going to take a shower and go to bed."

Brandon held her, and played with her hair, kissing her cheeks but she wasn't in a playful mood. He didn't get it. She said she felt better than ever but she didn't want more than being held.

After holding her for a half hour, she turned and kissed him. "Thanks honey. I'm going to shower and hit the sack. If you want to go out its okay with me. Just don't be too late."

"Okay. Hopefully tomorrow we'll both be a little better, maybe with no ghosts."

9

He sat down on a rocking chair; nobody was out on the porch which made him feel better. He didn't want to seem like a fool to the people they had just met. Hopefully Steve and Mary wouldn't think him a wacko and send him and JoAnne packing. Lost in his thoughts he drifted off to sleep.

He woke up and looked at his watch figuring he must have slept for about an hour. The little nap refreshed him and he hoped things would go back to normal. Perhaps paranormal activities might have ended with the sighting of her father's spirit, although he really didn't believe it.

He heard footsteps approaching and wasn't happy that he'd have to interact with anyone, but he'd say whatever needed to be said."

Steve sat down beside him. "I heard about your episode down at the beach. You could have seen a submarine because one was sunk during the war. Did you happen to see a number on it?"

"Yeah, I did. I'm pretty sure it was U-352."

"From what I read, there was a U-boat sunk about twenty-five miles off the coast, so that could have been the one you saw."

"You don't think I'm crazy, then?"

"No, Brandon. I don't. I've seen it too. I don't know why so many of my guests have seen it, but…" He took a sip of his drink. "There are plenty of ghost stories to go around in North Carolina. One may have even been up to mischief in one of my rooms. Years ago, a renter told me that she felt herself being pulled out of bed by her feet. She screamed and the feeling was gone. She called me in the middle of the night and told me what happened. I told her to try to go back to sleep. She called me and told me it happened again and she was not going to stay in that room any longer. I had a few vacancies, so I put her in another room and everything was fine. So was it a ghost? I don't know, but I don't misbelieve. "

"Interesting."

Steve got up. "I saw the soldier today. I assume you know him?"

Brandon shook his head. "I never met him, but I'm pretty sure it was JoAnne's dad. She told me she felt like a weight was lifted from her and I think she's going to be okay."

"Well, good luck to you both. If anything else strange happens, please let me know. Goodnight."

"Night, Steve."

He sat for a few more minutes and then went up to bed.

Southport, North Carolina
Wrightsville Beach, North Carolina, Morning

1

When Brandon awakened, he smelled coffee brewing and heard water running; JoAnne was in the shower. He eased himself into a sitting position on the edge of the bed, and found the remote control. He pointed it at the small flat screen TV attached to the wall a couple of feet from the end of the bed. A few moments later the screen lit up and Brandon tapped 6, changing the station to WECT. The news was on and the weather report would be coming up soon. He stood up, stretched, and walked to the kitchen. Opening the refrigerator, he grabbed the bread bag, took out two slices and set them on the small countertop. He opened the peanut butter jar, dug a knife in deeply and then spread one slice of bread with about a quarter of an inch of peanut butter. He placed the other slice on top, completing his breakfast sandwich and then took a healthy bite. As he chewed, he grabbed a cup, and then put a spoonful of creamer and a packet of sweet and low in the hot coffee. He stirred it, but before taking a sip, he added a little water from the tap. The aroma filled his nostrils and after he drank the first full cup and ate half of his sandwich, he began feeling much better.

He heard the water being turned off and he filled a cup for JoAnne. She liked it hot and black, but she always needed her shower before coffee. He walked into the bathroom and saw her drying herself. With her wet hair, both high and low, glistening with water beads, she just looked so sexy and he wanted her more than anything. She dropped the towel to the floor, and he handed her the cup. She nodded her thanks and then took a couple of sips. He was holding the remainder of his peanut butter sandwich and when she saw it she opened her mouth and he stuffed it in. While she chewed, he began to strip which made her smile.

When he was naked, and she finished the cup of coffee, he squeezed by in the tiny bathroom and slapped her ass before stepping into the very large shower. She stepped in with him and after drawing the shower curtain, she washed him, paying extra special attention to his manhood.

He backed her against the wall, entered her and they made love, roughly and quickly. It was over in a few minutes and then she showered again.

Planning to spend the day in Southport, they were on the road by eight. Brandon smiled because it was hard to get JoAnne moving unless they were on vacation or going shopping for clothes and jewelry.

The morning was beautiful, although there was a forty percent chance of showers predicted. Both of them were quietly taking in the sights along the road, and they both apparently saw the sign at the same time. As couples often do, they blurted out in unison, "Let's take the ferry."

JoAnne laughed and Brandon just smiled. "It's been a while since we said the same thing together," she said.

He nodded. "Yeah. I guess no situation came up that prompted simuspeak." He remembered the first time he coined that word. They had only been together a couple of months and after an extremely tense scene in the movie they were watching, they uttered the same words at the same time. They gave each other high fives and that's when he made up the word. She liked it a lot.

They got to the Fort Fisher Terminal with just enough time to purchase a ticket for the ferry leaving in less than five minutes. Brandon drove his car onto the boat, killed the engine and stepped on to the deck to stretch his legs.

2

JoAnne grabbed the camera and headed up to the bow to take some pictures. She had taken a bunch already, one of the first being a shot of the slot machine where she won most of her money. She had taken a picture of the room in Virginia, but when she looked at it, the photo was smoky. She wanted to show it to Brandon, but she forgot. She clicked back through the pictures until she found the shot and nearly dropped the camera. Sitting on their bed was a shadowy figure that certainly was not there when she first looked at the picture on Tuesday evening.

She had to lean against the side of the boat and she nearly fell over, but an older man managed to keep her upright.

"Are you okay, miss?" His gray eyes showed concern as he spoke through a mouth nearly covered by his drooping mustache.

When she looked at him a little closer, she was amazed and began to say, "Are you…?"

"Fluff Cowen. No, but I guess I bear a close resemblance to him. I don't even play golf." Fluff, whose first name is Mike, is the caddy for touring professional Jim Furyk. "What happened to you? Dizzy spell?"

Not wanting to share, she answered, "No, I guess I just don't have my sea legs working. Thanks for helping me, mister. It would have been embarrassing to fall down."

He smiled at her again: his eyes, which now appeared to be much darker than they were moments ago, seemed to stare right through her. She felt a chill, until he spoke again.

"No problem, but I need to tell you something very important." He paused for a moment. "Don't let him go on the ship." He turned and walked away and inexplicably vanished.

She blinked, but he was gone. She hurried back along the side of the boat, seeing Brandon wearing that thousand yard stare again.

Wondering if she should say anything to him, she decided not to because he was worked up enough. She took another look at the picture with the shadowy figure and the image had changed again. Now she was looking at the person or apparition she had just spoken to. He was staring straight toward her. His mouth was turned down and his eyes looked extremely sad. He was holding a piece of paper and she could see writing on it, but it was too small to read. She shrugged her shoulders, not even frightened anymore, and figured the words would get larger when she was supposed to read the note.

She waved and smiled when she saw Brandon look toward her. He smiled back.

3

Brandon drove the car off the ferry and headed toward town. He was looking forward to having a lobster roll and a couple of beers, while JoAnne wanted to visit as many of the stores as possible. They had dinner reservations in Wrightsville later and she didn't want to waste a minute.

Since it was a little too early for lunch, Brandon drove up Howe Street and JoAnne pointed out where she wanted to shop. There were several gift shops within a four block area; Artistry, Boo & Roo's and Chicks By The Sea were three places she wanted to peruse.

"I'd like to go to lunch around one if that's okay with you, Jo?"

She looked at her watch. "Yeah, that should be good. I'll meet you back at the car around noon. I might see some interesting shop on the way to lunch. If I'm running late, I'll call your cell. What are you going to do?"

"I think I'm just going to walk around a little. I'd like to see some of the places that were used in *Safe Haven* and *Under The Dome*. I know you didn't care for Dome, but we both liked *Safe Haven*."

"Okay, have fun," she said over her shoulder. "Don't get lost."

He flipped her the finger as she disappeared into a shop.

Once she was inside, she took a deep breath and looked at the picture again. The message was now easy to read, but she didn't know what it meant.

4

Brandon wandered around, watching people going about their business. It seemed like there were quite a few tourists because he saw license plates from seven different states within a block. Many of the people, especially women, were carrying shopping bags, and men, presumably husbands or boyfriends, were loading packages and shopping bags into cars. It appeared as though the Southport economy was doing pretty well.

He watched an elderly woman pushing a stroller. Since younger people were not present, he was concerned because she seemed rather frail and the stroller was quite small, giving him the indication of a very small child inside. Every minute or so she would reach into the stroller and smile, but one time she screamed. She pulled her hand back from the stroller and yelled: "How dare you scratch me like that. You'll pay later little man."

Hearing this, Brandon became quite concerned for the welfare of the child and he raced toward the woman before she could do anything to harm him.

She saw him coming toward her and shook her finger. "Stay away, young man. This is none of your business."

She stood beside the stroller, blocking his view, but he gently pushed her aside. He looked into the stroller and saw a large striped cat. He looked up at her and she laughed.

"I told you it was none of your business. I often take my cat out in the stroller and occasionally I get scratched. I

29

think you have more to worry about than me." She cackled and pushed the stroller quickly down the street.

A man nearby said, "Don't worry about her, mister. She scares the crap out of a lot of folks visiting. Most of us are used to her and we let her be."

He didn't understand what she meant by that remark, so he shrugged it off. He walked north on Howe for several blocks and then turned left, meandering down the pavement, looking at some neat homes. After he turned a corner he saw a young woman in a yard near a flagpole a couple of houses up the street. As he got closer, he saw that she was very attractive with long, brown hair that she was tying into a ponytail. She was wearing a swimming cover up and when she removed it, she was clad in very tiny black spandex shorts and a red tube top. She had long legs, but for a girl her height, which he thought was about five feet nine, she had dainty feet. She was barefoot, but a pair of flip flops were lying near her cover up.

She noticed him looking at her and smiled. She motioned him closer so he came to the white picket fence surrounding the yard and stopped.

"Hi. I'm Nicole and I'm an exotic dancer. I'm about to practice some of my moves on our flagpole if you'd like to watch. I'm going to try a few tricks I've never done and I think if I have an audience, even of one, I'll be able to concentrate harder. Do you mind?" Her killer smile and dancing eyes just roped him in all the way.

"Sure. I'll watch you, but I don't have any dollar bills." He laughed and she laughed right back.

"That's okay. No charge for today's performance and I really think you will like my ending. "

She placed her hands on the thin, sturdy pole and began climbing, wrapping her legs around it and slowly working her way upward toward the top. The pole was about fifteen feet high and it slightly swayed as she moved upward. When she was nearly at the top, she stretched out her legs and began to spin around and then worked her way down to about the halfway point. She stretched out again and in a moment she was hanging upside down, turning around the pole and making scissors movements with her legs, working her way down until she nearly touched the ground. She stretched her body nearly straight out, parallel to the ground and then swung once around the pole still parallel to the ground.

Brandon marveled at her strength and smoothness of movements and applauded. "You go, girl. Awesome!" He cried out.

After a few more amazing acrobatic movements, she climbed the pole to about the midway point and once again stretched straight out. She grabbed a lanyard attached to the tube strapped to her leg. Cloth began to stream straight down to the ground and he looked at it closely.

The top part of the cloth approximated half of an American flag. Right below that was a picture of what he thought was the battleship North Carolina. Below that was the message 'Don't Go to the Ship' and directly below that was what appeared to be a street address.

Brandon was shocked and then stunned when the girl, the cloth and the pole disappeared before his eyes.

He sat down hard, but he burned the address into his memory. It had to mean something.

5

JoAnne reread the message again. The gold is not where they thought. She had no idea what to think about that, but she figured it must have something to do with the North Carolina. *Who are they and whose gold is it? Were she and Brandon supposed to find this gold?* Yet she was told by the man on the ferry not to go to the ship. So many strange things were happening and she hoped she would be strong enough to see them through it. She was really concerned about her husband.

When they met up, neither told the other what happened to them.

He was standing by the car when she walked down the street carrying several shopping bags. He popped open the trunk and she put them inside.

As he closed it, he said, "Looks like you had a pretty good day shopping."

"Yeah, I did. I saved over two hundred dollars."

He laughed. It was a running gag between them. He never asked how much she spent, only how much she saved.

"What did you do while I was saving your money?" She inquired as she sat in the car and pulled the seat belt across her body and locked it.

He began backing out. "Not too much. I just took a walk around to see if I could find some of the places where they have filmed in town. I only saw one home that was used in *Safe Haven*. There are a lot of beautiful homes down here."

"Yeah, I bet there are. I could use a beer. How 'bout we find a cool place to get a drink?"

"Sounds good. I remember reading something about a restaurant called The Pharmacy. We could try that."

"Okay, let me check through a couple of brochures to find the address."

Brandon was driving back toward the center of town as JoAnne looked for the address.

"Found it. You gotta drive all the way to the end of town to Moore Street but I don't know if we need to turn left or right."

He laughed. "I guess we'll find it soon enough. The town sure isn't very big."

A few minutes later, he guessed correctly, turning right and soon they saw it. He parked and they hopped out the car, both of them laughing, feeling so good, and momentarily forgetting about their recent paranormal experiences.

When they saw the restaurant, they were really impressed. The façade was painted white with a black and white awning stretched out across most of the building. Two wrought iron tables each with two matching chairs flanked the doorway. They opened the door and stepped inside.

The restaurant stretched out in front of them, the entire wall on the right hand side was brick from floor to ceiling. At the back of the room was a fireplace. To their left was a cozy bar where they sat on wooden chairs.

A waitress appeared in front of them. "Hi, my name is Denise. How may I help you?"

JoAnne said. "I'll have a Blue Moon and my husband will have a Yuengling."

"Would you care to see a menu?"

"No thanks," Brandon replied. "We're going to go to Fishy Fishy for lobster lolls in about an hour or so."

"I like that place. About three years ago they transformed it into Porter's Stowaway Tavern when they filmed the pilot of *Revenge* here. Eventually the production moved to LA, but while the cast was here, our business really picked up. I think the Southport and Wilmington areas are fast becoming the Hollywood of the east."

When Denise walked toward the refrigerator, JoAnne turned around and looked at the people dining. The food did smell wonderful, but Brandon had his heart set on lobster rolls and now she wanted to see a former movie set too. . She turned back toward the bar just as their beers arrived. She took a sip which turned into several swallows, enjoying the flavor of the beer. "That is so refreshing."

He nodded after taking a couple of healthy swallows himself. "I sure do like my Vitamin Y."

They drank quietly for a few minutes, both of them lost in thought when two more beers were placed in front of them.

Looking at Denise quizzically they were confused not having ordered another. "This is from the gentleman and young lady sitting back there." She pointed behind them.

They turned and stared at the man from the ferry and the pole dancer and dropped their bottles on the floor.

When she heard the bottles break, Denise turned toward Brandon and JoAnne. They were staring at the table where the old man and the young woman were seated only moments ago. She was pretty sure that only about thirty seconds passed since she saw them sitting there. It was hard to believe that they could have walked out in that short period of time, without paying their check.

She hurried out from behind the bar and saw that the couple appeared to be in a state of shock, but she had to try to catch up with the couple that possibly stuck her with the check.

Racing out from the front door, she saw a man sitting at one of the outdoor tables, working on his laptop. "Excuse me, sir, but did you see a bearded man and a young woman come out from the restaurant?"

He turned his face toward her. "No, I didn't see anyone but I'm sure they could not have passed by without me hearing them." His dark sunglasses hid his eyes.

It was at that moment that she noticed a dog lying by the man's feet and a folded cane was on the table beside his computer. "Oops," she blurted out before even realizing it.

He smiled. "I guess you've figured out that I am blind."

"Yes, I did and I'm so sorry for jumping to conclusions."

"No problem." He stuck out his hand. I'm Richard Conlen." When he felt the dog rise and place his head on his leg, he ruffled his German Shepard's hair. "This is Riley."

She took his hand in hers and felt a jolt of electricity. The tingle actually felt good and she squeezed his hand a little tighter.

"You have a pretty good grip, miss...."

She released his hand. "I'm so sorry, Richard. Sometimes I forget how strong I am. My name is Denise Scott."

So, strongwoman Denise, why do you need to find the couple you think just left?"

"Well, they bought drinks for a couple sitting at the bar. When they dropped their bottles on the floor, I noticed the two people who bought the drinks were gone. What puzzles me is how quickly they disappeared. Oh, shit! Excuse me for that. I need to get back inside and clean up the mess and look after my customers. Can I get you anything?"

"Yeah. Any kind of beer will be fine. Surprise me."

"Okay, I'll be back out in a few minutes." As she walked back inside, she had a feeling she was going to be connected to something that would scare the hell out of her, or bring out the best of what she had to offer. She paused in front of Brandon and JoAnne. *Or both? God, what can I be getting into here?*

"Are you guys okay?' She asked as she bent down to pick up up the larger pieces of glass, just as a busser came over with a pan and brush. She stood back up as she watched him take care of the mess in short order.

"Thanks, John," she said as he walked back toward the kitchen.

Brandon finally looked at her. "Yeah, I think we're okay. I'm not quite sure what happened there."

JoAnne nodded. "Denise, I'm so sorry for making that mess."

Don't worry about it. I don't know where those people got to, but hopefully they'll come back and pay for those drinks."

Brandon pulled out his wallet and handed her a twenty.

"This should take care of it, plus the mess we made."

She waved him off. "I can't take your money. It's not your responsibility."

He put the bill back in his wallet. "Thanks. I guess we're going to head out."

"Well, have a good day. See you soon."

He paused for several moments. "Yes, I think you will."

After they left, she told her boss she was going on break and stepped back outside carrying two bottles of beer.

8

They walked, hand in hand, not saying anything for a long time. When JoAnne spotted a small park with some benches she guided Brandon toward one and they sat down. She squeezed his hand and said, "I guess I'll start."

She told him about the man on the ferry and what he said to her. "I know you want to go on the North Carolina tomorrow, honey, but I am so afraid something will happen to you."

He nodded and then told about the pole dancer. He was so animated that she had to laugh. But when he turned serious, she nodded.

"When the cloth unfurled, I was very impressed, and then I saw the address printed on the cloth. I think we need to go there."

She gripped his arm, not having told him that she had seen the same address in the picture that she took in the hotel. She pulled out the camera to show him, and there was no man and no paper with an address on it. "I know what I saw, Brandon. There was a man sitting on our bed, actually the same man who was on the ferry and in the restaurant and he was holding a paper with the same address on it."

"The map of Southport is back in the car. Let's see if

36

that address is in town. I think we need to go wherever it is."

They walked to the car and got in.

9

Denise sat down at the table. "Richard, I've brought your beer."

He reached for it and she put it in his hand. He took a sip. "Interesting. What brand is it?" He took another sip.

"It's Highland Pale Ale. I've grown very fond of it over the past year." She took a big swallow and burped. "OMG, excuse me, Richard."

"It's okay, Denise. I've been known to do that once or twice. Once I let one fly while I was questioning a witness and I thought the entire courtroom was going to bust out in laughter." He took a swallow. "Fortunately, they didn't, and I got right back into the line of questioning."

"Wait a minute. You're a blind attorney? I didn't even know there were blind lawyers."

"Well, it's often said that justice is blind, so I thought, what the hell, give it a shot, Rick."

"Have you been blind from birth?"

"No. I lost my sight in a skiing accident when I was about fourteen." He paused momentarily, wiping his eyes. "I was devastated. I had big plans to become a professional skier, but I just couldn't picture myself flying down hills without being able to see where I was going. I used to listen to television with my folks and the thought struck me that I could definitely be a lawyer.

"I talked it over with my mom and dad and they were supportive. After I graduated from high school, with a four point oh, I applied to a bunch of law schools and I was finally accepted by St. Mary's University. I got my law degree in five years and I worked for a couple of firms up north until last month. Hung my shingle down here and I'm working hard to build my business."

She was mesmerized, but not necessarily with his story. As he was speaking, she looked him over and really liked what she saw. In a nutshell he was gorgeous with wavy, brown hair, and a very handsome face. He used his hands when he spoke and they appeared soft and gentle.

He was waiting for a response, but none was forthcoming. "Ah, Denise, are you still on planet earth?"

"Sorry, Rick. I was listening, but I'm still thinking about those two people that stiffed me."

"What do you remember about them?"

"That's the odd thing. I don't recall them being there at all until the man raised his hand to get my attention. I went to the table and they had drinks in front of them, but I can't remember anyone serving them."

"That is odd. Do you remember what they said to you?"

She looked at him. "It sounds as though you are questioning me, counselor."

"My bad. I get that way sometimes and it drives my friends crazy. May I rephrase your honor?"

"Not necessary. The man looked very familiar, but I haven't been able to pin it down. The woman was stunning and she was muscular, like she was a dancer or something. I'd say he was around sixty and she could have been 30. Possibly a December May relationship. I don't think he was her dad, but they could have just been friends. Anyway he said, 'Miss, would you please get that young couple at the bar a drink on me. I'll settle up later.'

"I brought them the beers, told them they were from the gentleman and lady behind them. I went about my business and then next thing I knew I heard glass breaking. I just don't remember anything else."

"Maybe the couple knew them and didn't expect to see them here. I wonder if we'll ever find out."

"My guess is we will sooner than later."

"How? Are you psychic?"

"No, the woman, whose name is JoAnne Pederson,

forgot her purse. I'm looking at her license now."

When they arrived at Fishy Fishy, JoAnne looked in the back seat and didn't see her purse. "Brandon, we need to go back to The Pharmacy, I think I left my purse there. I know I had it when I walked in, but after seeing those people, phantoms, or whatever, I guess I just forgot to grab it before we left. I was a little shook up."

He turned the car around and drove back.

He found the same parking space and saw Denise sitting outside with the guy who was there when they left. Denise lifted the purse high in the air and JoAnne smiled.

As they started to walk across the street, the skies opened up. One of the famous North Carolina storms was there before anyone even realized what was coming. They raced for the restaurant, and in moments they were under cover.

Denise was helping Rick with his laptop. When everything was gathered, the foursome stepped inside. Riley stood by the door and whined, but he wasn't invited in, so he curled up as close to the door as possible.

Denise handed JoAnne her purse and then stepped behind the bar. "What can I get you guys? I don't think you want to go back out in this storm."

"Allow me to buy this round," Rick offered. "It seems like you two didn't have a very good day." He put out his hand. I'm Rick Conlen."

When Brandon went to shake his hand, he noticed that Rick didn't respond. "Hi Rick. I'm Brandon Pederson and this is my wife JoAnne." He took Rick's hand and shook it.

"Cat's out of the bag. You figured out that I'm blind." He chuckled.

Brandon laughed. "Yeah, you can't fool me, pal."

"Have you been blind since birth? "JoAnne inquired

Rick told her the skiing story and how he became an attorney. "So if you ever need a good lawyer, give me a call." He handed her his card.

They each drank two beers and by the time they finished, the storm was nearly over. After JoAnne went to the bathroom, the rain had stopped.

Brandon stood up. "JoAnne and I have to head back to Wrightsville Beach, but we're going to grab a lobster roll first. We have dinner plans and want to get a little rest before we head out tonight. Rick and Denise, it was so nice meeting you both. I sure will keep you in mind, Rick, in the event I get arrested and need a lawyer."

JoAnne gave him a weird look, but didn't say anything.

Several minutes after leaving, she closed her eyes and fell asleep.

Brandon wondered what tomorrow would bring, but he hoped that whatever happened, he and his wife would make it through and become stronger than ever.

Thursday, June 19th, 2014

Wrightsville Beach. Afternoon And Evening

1

Nobody was on the back porch when they returned. The parking lot was empty, so it seemed like everyone was out enjoying some facet of being at the beach.

They went up to their apartment and flopped down on the bed.

Brandon kissed JoAnne and stroked her hair. He could see fear in her eyes and he needed to comfort her. "I don't know why our ghosts don't want me to go to the ship. I think if I go, I might be able to get some answers."

She nodded. "I understand how important going there must be, but I am really scared, Brandon. There have been so many unexplainable events and if we'd even talk to any of our friends or relatives, they'd think we lost our minds."

"Steve and I talked last night and I think we should talk to him together after dinner. At least he won't laugh at us. Speaking of dinner, would you be interested in an appetizer my dear." He moved his eyebrows go up and down which always made her laugh.

The tension was broken and they made love, slowly at first and then with an urgency that made both of them gasp in pleasure. When they finished, they held on to each other for a long time, kissing, allowing time for their breathing to return to normal.

Brandon sat up on the edge of the bed, looked at her and smiled. "I'm getting pretty hungry, honey bunny, what say we take a shower and head out for dinner."

"Sounds good to me. Maybe we'll come back and have some dessert." She smiled devilishly.

2

They walked hand in hand up to the South Beach Grill. Boats were cruising up and down the sound. Some people were fishing from the shore. At one pier, a large group of people were partying and the scents of grilled meat only whetted their appetites for the evening meal. The sun, a large white orb, hovered over the sound and by the time they would be heading back to the apartments, it would be setting in a cloudless sky.

The restaurant was pretty busy and they would have to wait twenty to thirty minutes for a table, but they didn't care. They ordered drinks; JoAnne had a glass of Trapiche Malbec, a wine from Argentina-Red plum and cherry aromas, soft hints of spice with a touch of oak, and a long, sweet finish. Brandon had a glass of Red Oak Amber lager, brewed in North Carolina.

They sipped at their drinks, watching the traffic on the sound and enjoying the music coming from the speakers. It was a great way to spend an evening.

Once they were seated, they ordered another drink and chose Crab and Seafood Nachoes for Two. When the drinks and appetizers arrived they ordered their meals. JoAnne ordered Grouper Linda and Brandon chose Smoked Chicken Tortellini.

Their waitress, Sherrl Wilhide, heard them mention Wilkes Barre and said, "I lived in Pittston when I was a kid and moved down here about fifteen years ago. I love it, had to get my dainty feet into the water more often than one week a year."

JoAnne nodded. "I think someday I would like us to live at the beach too. This is such a nice area, and people are so friendly."

Brandon looked down at Sherrl's sneakers and saw how small they were. She wasn't kidding when she said she had dainty feet.

"Is this your first visit to Wrightsville Beach?"

"Yeah," Brandon answered. "My granddad served on the North Carolina and I've been wanting to see his ship for years. We're going there tomorrow."

"I went on it once. It's a little eerie below deck and some guy wrote a book about the ghosts of the North Carolina."

JoAnne and Brandon stared at her, not knowing that fact.

"Well, I better get about my business. I'll be back to check on you guys later."

She hustled away and JoAnne said, "This stuff is really getting freaky, Brandon." He nodded and they started eating their meals.

As they ate, they talked about all the things that had happened to them so far on this trip, both dreading, yet looking forward to, what tomorrow would bring. Brandon brought a forkful of food up to his mouth and dropped the fork, seeing the old man and the pole dancer walking down the path across the street. They both nodded at him.

JoAnne spotted them at the same time but surprisingly, she did not get upset and wondered why. She took out her iPhone and centered them in the screen. One press and there was a clear picture of nobody. "Well, they didn't photograph." Weird, since the old man showed up on her phone before. She shrugged thinking that if a ghost wanted to be photographed, it could be; if not, well….

Brandon had calmed down. "Why do we keep seeing them? The address they gave us was a vacant lot."

She shrugged, taking another sip of wine. "Maybe the lot wasn't always vacant. I think they want us to find out what was there at one time and maybe then they'll leave us alone."

"Google the address and see what you come up with."

She keyed in the address and found 17,200 possibilities with that number and street. She scrolled a couple of pages and didn't find anything specific. "I wonder if that blind lawyer could help us with this. He seemed really nice."

"I don't know, honey, but I guess it couldn't hurt to contact him. You have his card, right?"

"Yeah, I do. I'll give him a call after we finish dinner and we're walking back to the Inn."

<h1 style="text-align:center">3</h1>

Rick was in his office, working on an estate case, but his mind kept wandering back to what happened earlier. He saw the old man and the young girl leave The Pharmacy and as soon as they were beside his table, they both stared at him in amazement.

He never told anyone that he could communicate with the dead and he wanted to keep it that way. Being blind in a sighted world, especially in his line of work, was tougher than he could ever have imagined, but he truly believed he would become successful.

Both ghosts nodded at him and then disappeared just as Denise came out the door. He had a feeling it would not be the last time he would see them and he was pretty sure he had not seen the last of Brandon and JoAnne either.

Time was his enemy on this case; he seemed to never have enough time for research and preparation, and when the phone rang, he thought twice about answering. Knowing that if he didn't answer, he could lose a prospective client, he picked up on the fourth ring. "Richard Conlen Law Office", he said.

"Mr. Conlen. This is JoAnne Pederson. How are you?"

"Busier than a one-armed paper hanger, but what can I do for you?"

She smiled at his humor, liking him more and more since they met yesterday. "I was wondering if you could find out who used to live at 941 East Moore Street. Several, uh, people gave us this address and told us to go there, but we don't know why we were sent to a vacant lot."

"I think I can find out who lived there in the past, but

it might take a day or two."

It took her awhile to respond and Rick could hear muffled voices. She must have covered the phone with her hand. "Well, that would probably be okay, but is there any chance at all that we could get that information by tomorrow around noon at the latest."

"I'll give it my best shot, Mrs. Pederson, but I can't make any promises. Denise from The Pharmacy is coming over a little later and I can ask her to help me out. Best I can do for you."

"That's fine. We'll look forward to hearing from you."

He thought she sounded disappointed as she hung up the phone.

He turned his head both ways and saw five ghosts standing in his office. Putting his work aside, he said, "How can I help you all today?"

4

When they returned to the Inn, the two couples they had already met were sitting on the porch having drinks and enjoying a lively conversation with Steve and Mary. Another couple they had not met was sitting on the love seat by the wall. They didn't really want to get into a conversation, but they didn't want to be rude, so Brandon asked if anyone would like a beer. JoAnne sat down as he went up to the room to grab three bottles.

He came back down, handing beers to JoAnne and Chuck.

Mary said to him, "So where did you and JoAnne go today?"

"We drove to Fort Fisher and took the ferry to Southport."

Sara said, "Rich and I went there yesterday. What a really neat town."

"Yeah, it is," JoAnne chimed in. "There are so many really cool shops there. We had drinks at The Pharmacy and lobster rolls at Fishy Fishy."

Rich nodded. "We pretty much did the same thing. I was so impressed with the number of movies and TV shows that were shot in Southport and Wilmington. I guess this area is fast becoming the Hollywood of the east."

"Yeah. I found a home that was used in the movie, *Safe Haven*," Brandon responded. He also told them about the lady with the cat in the baby carriage. It took forever for the laughter to die down.

As Brandon was telling everyone the cat story, Steve saw two spirits sitting on the railing. He didn't say anything. Neither Brandon nor JoAnne saw them, and he was hoping they wouldn't. Steve just kept an eye on them as everyone began to ask questions about the cat, Southport, and the ferry. Brandon and JoAnne never glanced toward the specters and several minutes later they just vanished.

By ten-thirty, all of the guests had gone to bed, so Steve turned off the lights and called it a night himself.

Friday, June 20th, 2014

Wilmington, North Carolina

1

After an amazing breakfast at the Causeway Café where they ate fried green tomatoes for the very first time, they drove into the city of Wilmington where JoAnne had some huge shopping plans and Brandon was pretty much there as a chauffeur and package carrier until his wife grew tired of shopping or she decided that she had spent enough money.

He parked the car in the lot and then put a folded five dollar bill in a slot of the pay station corresponding to the numbered space on the lot. He had to push the bill all the way through with a small metal tool. Once that function was completed, he was paid up for a full day.

They walked hand in hand and as soon as the great battleship came into view, Brandon started to experience a pulling sensation, as though someone had grabbed hold of his arm and was trying to guide him closer the North Carolina. He kept fighting the feeling, wondering that if he ever boarded the ship, he might possibly die.

JoAnne hooked her arm through his other arm, but she could feel the pull as well and the feeling was extremely uncomfortable. "Brandon, the ghosts don't want to you to go the ship. Please don't go, honey."

He was sweating profusely so she steered him to a bench where they both sat down for a few minutes. Neither of them said a word and soon Brandon was feeling better and he just wanted her to finish shopping so they could leave and go somewhere else.

He turned around and looked toward the ship. He could see sailors dressed in World War II style navy uniforms standing on the deck and sitting on the wings of the airplane. Visitors were oblivious to their presence and just continued to look over the ship and take pictures. One of the sailors waved to him and he waved back.

JoAnne watched her husband, not knowing who he was waving to, because none of the visitors on the ship seemed to be waving.

"Who are you waving to, honey?' She inquired.

"There are ghost sailors over there." He kept staring at one who stepped forward. "It's him. It's my granddad." He grabbed her shoulders roughly and when he spoke his tone was menacing. "He wants me to come over to the ship and talk to him. He wants to tell me who killed him. I gotta go, JoAnne."

Brandon let her go and then started to run to the car with her in hot pursuit.

"Honey, please stop!" She yelled as his lead lengthened.

He just kept running, either because he didn't hear her or he was ignoring her.

She gained a few steps when Brandon had to stop because he couldn't make it across the street since several cars were coming toward him, exceeding the speed limit.

When he was able to run again, she was only fifteen feet behind him and the parking lot was less than a half a block away. She dug into her purse and pulled out her set of car keys. As soon as she saw the lights flash, signifying that the car was now unlocked, she hit the lock button with hers, denying him access. She did this twice before he caught on and he stared at her. The hatred she saw was nothing like she had ever seen before and she became afraid of him. She stopped and put her car keys back in her purse as he climbed behind the wheel, started the car and drove away. All she would be able to do would be to wait for him to come back. If he didn't, she would get a cab and head back to the beach. She didn't know if she would stay and wait for him, or find a way back to Wilkes Barre.

Brandon drove across the bridge over the Cape Fear River and picked up the main highway leading to Battleship Row. He was nearly in a trance, the pull of his grandfather's spirit becoming greater the closer he got to the battleship. When he turned onto USS North Carolina Road, he was feeling morose, and yet he was filled with an inexplicable joy as he looked toward the ship. He parked the car and opened the trunk, lifting the floor that hid the spare tire, but the spare tire was no longer there. Instead, there was a small duffle bag containing one of Al Pederson's World War Two navy work uniforms. Brandon quickly slipped out of his clothes and stood there wearing a white t shirt, white boxers, and blue socks. Nobody was nearby when he disrobed. He then put on the light blue chambray work shirt, navy blue dungarees, black work shoes, a black web belt with a brass buckle and then he finished the look with a white navy cap, known as a Dixie Cup. The cap could be squared, rolled, crushed, fitted with "gull wings" or simply worn as designed. It could also be used as a flotation device or a sun shield or even, some claim, as a dog food dish. With its many shapes and uses, it was probably the most versatile article of clothing a Navy enlisted man wore.

He closed the trunk and then headed for the battleship. When he paid to go on board, the cashier said, "Very authentic looking uniform, young man. It's always nice to see someone take the time to look the part before going on the ship."

"Thanks," Brandon said, smiling. "This uniform belonged to my grandfather and he served on this ship." Then his face grew darker and he uttered, "I was murdered on this ship."

"Excuse me?" the cashier inquired.

Brandon just offered him a mock salute and walked up the ramp to the ship. When his feet touched the North

Carolina, he saw a ghostly image coming toward him and he screamed. His head felt like it was going to explode and he fell to the deck.

Sunday, 18 June, 1944

On The Battleship North Carolina

1

Albert Pederson drew two cards, shuffled his hand, and then slowly fanned his cards open. On the extreme right was the ace of spades, as the second card was partially revealed he saw the ace of clubs. He worked the third card from beneath the second, and he saw the eight of spades. The next card was the eight of clubs.. Inwardly he smiled having drawn a dead man's hand with his first four cards. The hand got its name from a poker game involving Wild Bill Hickok. The game was stud poker, four cards up and one down. Bill had the two aces and two eights, which made him the probable winner of the game already. As he went to look at his hole card, he was shot dead and aces and eights became known as the dead man's hand. Al revealed the ace of diamonds as his fifth card.

Looking over the top of his cards at the other five players, he bet thirty dollars. Justin Nonnemacher, a twenty-four year old mailman, from Amarillo. Texas, a very good card player stared at him trying to get a read, but not seeing anything, folded. Jeff Ambrose, a twenty-two year old former Ohio State football star, tapped his cards on the floor a few times, took one more look and tossed them in. He nodded at Al and smiled. Twenty year old James Richman, a truck driver from Slatington, Pennsylvania, called. Carl Mantle, a twenty-seven year old professional boxer, with a record of forty-three wins to no losses, said, "I call." LeRoy 'Pops' Hamilton, called. He was called Pops because he was the oldest of the group at twenty-nine. Born in Elmira, New York, he was a plumber who lived in the Bronx. Al took long looks at his opponents. Each of them had taken two cards as well, so it was conceivable that one of them could have four of a kind. No one could have a higher full house. He pretty much ruled out any of his three challengers having a straight flush on a two card draw, but you never knew.

Carl picked up several chips, then added a couple more and said, "Raise you twenty, Al." He smiled and blinked his eyes twice. Albert then knew he had nothing because every time he blinked twice, he was a loser. He was trying to steal the pot.

Pops fanned his cards again, but they would not change and Al was pretty sure he didn't have a winner either. When he saw Pops bite his lip, Al was certain he had a smaller full house. He always bit his lip when he had a good hand. "Call your fifty, Carl and raise twenty." He laid his cards on the floor and lit a cigarette.

Jim continued to study his cards, looking into the eyes of his opponents, probably reading Carl, Al thought. He tossed in seventy dollars in cash and nodded. "Call. Up to you, Al."

"Well boys, I think I have you all beat, so I'm going to raise another thirty. Anyone game, or is that too steep?"

Carl folded. "Too rich for me, guys. I'm out." He stood up and jumped into his rack, ready to grab some shuteye.

Pops called and Jim added twenty more. Al debated on bumping it up another thirty but he didn't want to have his friends get too angry at him for winning as much as he did. There would be many days or nights to take these guys for more of their hard earned money. "Call you, Jim. What you got?"

Jim laid his hand on the floor; he had three queens and a pair of nines, a pretty nice full house. Pops couldn't beat that so he tossed his cards on top of the pile of chips and cash on the floor.

Jim was smiling from ear to ear and he was ready to pull all that money toward him when Al tossed his full house on top of the pot. "Sorry, pal, but I guess I win again."

His buddies stared at him and shook their heads. "How

the hell do you do it, Al? I know you ain't cheating, but to win so often is against all the odds ever made." Pops stood up. "I'm broke so it's time for this old man to hit the sack."

2

After he was sure his poker friends were sound asleep, Al quietly left the area and worked his way to the engine room. Petty Officer Harmon Elkland was sitting at his desk poring over some papers.

Al saw Harmon's head pop up and then turn toward him, a smile creasing his face. "I'm hoping you have a lot of money on you tonight, my friend."

"I do." He placed the stack of bills on the desk and waited while Elkland counted it up.

He whistled. "Wow, you certainly had a very good night tonight, Al. Six hundred and twenty-seven dollars will buy you three hundred and thirty dollars in gold coins. I'm running pretty low, so this will probably be the last time we'll be able to do business until I can get to my supplier." He got up and walked to his locker. He counted out the total in twenty dollar gold pieces and two five dollar pieces. He handed them to Al. "You must have over seven grand in coins now."

"Yeah, and you have almost fourteen grand in cash. If we don't die in this fuckin' war, we'll have a pretty good start when we get home."

Harmon nodded. "I still don't understand why you would pay twice the amount for gold, but that's certainly your business and I'm always happy to business with you."

"I'm a gambler, Harm, so I'm betting that after the war, the value of gold will shoot up and I'll have more money than I could earn in ten years. I want to live on easy street with Eleanor and my son." He paused for a moment, and then added, "I can't wait to see him. I've missed him being born and I might not see him for another year or more…if ever. I just have a feeling I'm not going to make it."

After shaking hands with Eckland, Al turned on his heel and headed back toward his working area. He looked both ways before taking the key from around his neck. He opened the small padlock, slid it through the two brackets and opened the hatch. Several months ago he had found a perfect void to hide his stash and he was certain that nobody had ever known this place existed. He recalled a friend of his telling him about a tiny cubby hole he found on his aircraft carrier; a place where he could be by himself for as much time as he needed to be alone. This spot wasn't big enough for a person to hide in, but it was perfect for his gold.

He stashed his winnings and went back outside, locking up behind him. He knew that nobody ever came here at night, and he never recalled anyone asking why the hatch was padlocked. Sometimes it was best not to ask any questions to a person of higher rank. To his knowledge the only sailors who used this passageway used it as a shortcut of sorts and probably never gave a padlocked hatch a second thought.

Al was a little concerned about the amount of money he was winning from his fellow sailors. Nobody knew about him exchanging the money for the gold coins and he was going to keep it that way. Scuttlebutt around the ship was that a battle was looming soon, perhaps as early as tomorrow. He didn't know if he or anyone on board would be alive after another battle, so he decided he better write a letter. A few minutes later he finished and stashed it in his small lock box. In the event of his death, his son would need to know where the gold was hidden so he could get it someday. If the ship would be sunk, nothing would matter at all, but he didn't think that would happen.

He returned to his sleeping area, climbed in his rack and was out in minutes.

After Al walked from the sleeping quarters, Jeff followed him at a discreet distance. He overheard the conversation between Al and the petty officer. He smiled, knowing that there was over seven thousand dollars in gold coins stashed somewhere and all he had to do was find it. When Al headed his way, he ducked behind some cardboard boxes and after Al passed, he followed him again.

Al stopped in the passageway. Jeff watched him closely, and before AL was able to turn around, Jeff found a place to hide. He peeked out and saw Al take a key from around his neck and open a tiny hatch. He withdrew a small canvas bag, which he then opened. He took a handful of gold coins from his shirt pocket and put them in the bag. Jeff ducked back again as he felt that Al was going to look in his direction. Moments later, Jeff once again peeked around the corner and he watched Al relock the hatch and then start to walk away.

Jeff waited a couple of minutes and then he cautiously strode to the little hatch. He tried the lock, hoping that Al may not have set it, but it was closed tight. He wondered if all of Al's gold was in this one place or if he had stashes elsewhere on the ship. Knowing Al though, Jeff was fairly certain that this void contained seven thousand dollars in gold coins and he was going to get all the money back that he had lost since assigned to this ship.

When he reentered the sleeping quarters, Al was already snoring. He entertained the thought of taking the key from around Al's neck now and then going back for the gold, but he decided to enlist additional help. He was going to talk to Pops in the morning.

Monday, 19 June, 1944

On The Battleship North Carolina

1

Task Force 58 was comprised of 129 naval vessels, which included twenty-eight submarines and fifteen carriers carrying 956 aircraft. The Americans were facing a Japanese force of 90 vessels which included nine carriers and twenty-four subs. The Japs had a total of 750 carrier based and land based aircraft. Before the battle, nicknamed the Marianas Turkey Shoot was over, Japan would lose nearly six hundred and fifty planes and three carriers. Japan would never be able to recover from these losses.

2

General quarters was sounded, immediately waking everyone who was asleep. The sailors hurriedly dressed and they were off to their battle stations, knowing that an engagement with the Japs was imminent. The North Carolina and six other fast battleships, plus eight heavy cruisers were deployed in front of the larger carriers to act as an anti-aircraft shield.

Jeff and Pops took their seats at their guns and waited. Five sailors, including Al, were ready to feed the two twin 40 millimeter guns.

Al was standing right behind the guns, checking out the sky. Off in the distance he saw tracers crisscrossing through the sky. The tracers seemed continuous but there were four rounds between each tracer.

Pops turned back to him. "It sure looks pretty, doesn't it, Al?"

"Yeah, it does, but there are an awful lot of bullets flying out there. I think we're gonna be damn busy in a short period of time. The sun will be up in less than a half hour and I imagine Jap planes aren't too far from this task force." Al looked at each man in the gun crew wondering how many of them would be alive after this battle was over. He focused a little longer on Larry Scott, the only one of the crew who would not play poker. He was a quiet kid from Southport, North Carolina. At nineteen years old, he didn't smoke nor would he take a drink. As the others played cards, he usually sat on the floor or laid in his bunk reading the bible. When Al saw Larry staring at him, he turned away. He hoped the kid would make it out of this mess. He went back to watching the sky.

3

Around 10:00 AM, the first Japanese aircraft were spotted approaching the task force and shortly after the big guns opened up, Jeff and Pops aimed the quad 40 millimeter antiaircraft guns and began firing as well. Jeff saw one plane coming in low and he could see the torpedo hanging on the bottom of the aircraft. Working the wheel, he lowered the guns and watched tracer rounds tear into the plane before the pilot was able to release the torpedo. The enemy plane exploded and pieces of it hit the North Carolina, causing little damage. Jeff heard the gun crew cheer his good shooting. He was glad they got that plane because had the torpedo been released, the battleship could have been sunk, ending his chance to get all of Al's gold. Of course, there was still the problem of getting rid of Al.

Jeff was becoming too busy to think about the gold as more and more Jap planes were circling the ships. They were met in the air by Hellcats and within minutes twenty-five enemy planes were shot down. The 40 millimeter gun crews shot down a few as well.

He saw Jap planes being shot down by U.S. aircraft and ships and it was a turkey shoot for sure. Looking up in the sky, the air was filled with contrails of American fighters.

Yet, even with the Japanese losing so many aircraft, they just kept coming and the gun crew was busy throughout the day.

Eventually, the Japs quit the fight and the men were able to go below decks, chow down, shower and get some sleep as the task force sailed west to find the Japanese fleet.

4

Al Pederson lay in his rack, so tired he could hardly keep his eyes open, but so afraid to sleep. He had noticed Jeff and Pops looking back at him several times during the day's battle and was sure that one or both of them were going to try to find out where the gold was hidden and more than that, he figured one or both of them were going to try to kill him. He stressed that in the note he had written and put in his lock box. If he didn't survive the war, he was certain that his personal gear would be shipped home to his family.

He saw a light and smiled, knowing that Larry had turned on his flashlight and was reading his Bible. Usually when this happened, it was pretty certain that most of the men had fallen asleep. He didn't know how Larry knew this, but he had never heard anyone cry out "turn off the fuckin' light already", like he used to hear during training, when he tried to catch up on the necessary reading to pass the classes the recruits had to take.

Al placed both hands behind his head and closed his eyes. The water was a little rough and he had noticed that the ship was moving pretty fast, causing it to bounce around in the water. Perhaps an hour later, he drifted off to sleep.

Tuesday, 20 June, 1944

On The Battleship North Carolina

After daybreak, the crew was awakened by a call to battle stations. When the 40 millimeter gun crews reported, Al Pederson was absent.

"Where the fuck is Pederson?" Chief Lamont bellowed.

The crew members looked around and then back at the chief, shrugging their shoulders.

"He better get his ass up here before too long, or there will be hell to pay. Did any of you guys sleep topside last night?"

They all shook their heads. Often sailors would sleep on deck because it was usually way too hot down below, but the last couple of nights hadn't been too bad.

After the chief left to check on other stations, Pops and Jeff talked quietly.

"Jeff, did you see Al last night?"

He nodded. "Pops, he was sound asleep and snoring like hell. A couple hours later, I saw he was gone. I figured he got restless and took a walk, but he never came back to bed. He should be here too, unless the dumb ass fell overboard. He was drinking quite a bit before he went to sleep. Maybe he was too drunk to keep his feet."

Pops shrugged. "Maybe mother nature took care of our job for us. Time will tell."

Both men went back to watching the sky for Jap planes, hoping today would not be as rough as yesterday.

The task force spent most of the day trying to find the Japanese fleet, but on the North Carolina, a large number of men were trying to find Al Pederson.

His gun team checked every area of the ship within a hundred feet of their guns, but Al couldn't be located anywhere. By the end of the day, the search was suspended and it was determined that Al had fallen overboard.

Later, Jeff found the key to the padlock lying on Al's

bunk. He took and went to the small void. When he was certain no one was coming, he inserted the key and turned. He removed the padlock, opened the little hatch and put his hand inside. After feeling around the entire space, there was no gold to be found. Who had it?

Friday, June 20th, 2014

The Battleship North Carolina

1

Brandon's screaming drew the attention of everyone within listening distance, even across the Cape Fear River.

JoAnne heard it and although she didn't know it was Brandon, she had a feeling that it was him for sure. She didn't know how to get there and as a crowd gathered nearby, she said, "My husband is over on that ship and he's been having some problems. I'm afraid the screams might be him. Is there any way I can get over there quickly?"

A policeman heard her and responded. "Ma'am, I can get you over there in a few minutes. I'll flag down the next water taxi for you." He turned toward the river and saw one coming. Waving his both arms, he shouted to the pilot.

The pilot guided the boat to the dock where the Cape Fear Riverboats stopped.

JoAnne stepped on board and the pilot took off across the river. Several minutes later he pulled up to the dock near the big ship.

He had radioed ahead and a park guide helped JoAnne up to the deck of the battleship.

Brandon was writhing on the deck, screaming his head off, but when he saw her he calmed down and smiled.

She knelt down and held him in her arms, soon hearing the wail of sirens. An ambulance was on the way. A few minutes later, the paramedics gently moved her aside and took Brandon's vital signs.

They loaded him into the back of the ambulance and helped JoAnne in as well and in moments they were headed to Veterans Memorial Hospital.

She watched as the paramedics continued checking his

vital signs and searching for anything that could be causing his screaming, which had started up again, shortly after the ambulance left the ship. He was given diazepam to calm him down. This helped to reduce the intensity of his screams, but they never did totally subside until after he was inside the hospital

2

He was taken to a holding room where JoAnne was able to sit with him.

Two nurses came in and as one took his blood pressure and pulse, the other inserted an IV into his other arm. He was being given intravenous injections of propofol and midazolam. The meds finally were working to calm him down even more and eventually he fell asleep.

JoAnne sat there watching him sleep for at least fifteen minutes when a doctor came in. He said, "I'm Doctor Carrington. Can you tell me what happened to your husband?" He began reading the patient chart.

"It's a long story, Doctor Carrington and I don't know if you'll believe me, but I think my husband is being possessed by the spirit of his grandfather." She stopped for a moment to let him absorb that information.

He had been checking Brandon's eyes and after listening to her, he stopped and looked into her eyes to see if she was trying to pull his leg.

She nodded her head.

"What would make you come to that conclusion?" He briefly looked at the chart again and took a seat next to her.

JoAnne explained everything that had been going on since they met, and even told him that she had felt a cold presence in their hotel room on Wednesday morning.

He listened intently and recommended that Brandon be admitted for observation.

"How long will he have to stay here?"

"At this time, I can't say, Mrs. Pederson. I have never had a patient with paranormal visitations." He stood up. "I'm going to stop the sedatives so we'll be able to talk to him in about two hours. In the meantime, I was about to go to the cafeteria for some coffee and a doughnut. Would you care to join me?"

"Yes, I would love a cup of coffee. Could you please tell me where the nearest restroom is before we go, and please call me JoAnne."

"The restroom is on the right, fifth door down. I'll be waiting outside for you. I'm Russ."

3

Shortly after JoAnne and Doctor Carrington left Brandon's room, a nurse came in to remove the sedative from the IV. She then proceeded to straighten out Brandon's sheet and blanket because he felt a little cold.

He opened his eyes and when he saw he was being looked after by a nurse, he inquired, "Nurse, where am I?"

She didn't realize he had awakened and she gasped. "Oh, Mr. Pederson, I'm sorry. You just startled me because I didn't expect you to awaken so quickly."

He looked around the room and his eyes grew wide. Very few things were recognizable and when he saw the flat screen TV, he was truly amazed and watched for a moment. He saw a man talking about the weather and at the bottom of the picture he saw the date, Friday, June 20; the time, and Wilmington. He started screaming again and the nurse called for security.

Two security officers hurried in just as Brandon Pederson tried to rip the IV from his arm. They held him down and the nurse ran out to get more help.

Three men in hospital whites rushed in and helped the security officers hold the patient down while the nurse paged Dr. Carrington.

Russ and JoAnne were drinking coffee, eating glazed doughnuts, and talking about Brandon and his problem.

"Russ, I am so afraid for him. When he left Wilmington to go to the North Carolina I very much considered going back to Wilkes Barre. Fortunately I knew that really wasn't an option I could take." She took a sip of coffee and a small bite of her doughnut. "I love him so much, but I don't know if he will ever get over this obsession."

"You said his grandfather, Al, disappeared at sea, but apparently the letter you both found in his personal effects revealed that several men could have been responsible for his death. I would imagine if he was murdered, the chances of finding his killer or killers will be extremely remote."

She dabbed her mouth with a napkin. "I agree. Not only that, but if there is no body, how can law enforcement people even open up a case. Plus, we don't know if any of the people named in the letter are alive."

"Didn't you guys do a Google search?"

"I didn't, and if Brandon did, he never told me."

"Do you remember any of the names?"

She thought hard for a few moments and then shook her head. "Nothing is coming to me. Sorry. I think Brandon might have brought the letter with him, though."

"I think it might be a good idea to see what you can come up with. If any of the sailors are alive, you could at least contact them and find out what they remember about Al Pederson's disappearance." He looked at his watch. "We better start heading up to see your husband."

Coincidental as it seemed, the overhead blared. "Dr. Carrington please report to the ER. Stat."

He and JoAnne quickly left the cafeteria to get back to Brandon.

Brandon struggled with the medical people trying to restrain him. They had strapped his legs at two places and one wrist was bound to the side rail. With his one free hand he managed to grab the hospital gown of a male nurse and pulled hard until the nurse's face was inches from him. "Don't do this to me," he cried out. "I need to get back to my ship." He lost consciousness, releasing his grip allowing the nurse to get the other restraint around his wrist and the rail.

At that moment, Dr. Carrington and JoAnne returned to the room.

She gasped when she saw her husband bound to the bed and quickly went to his side. She leaned over and kissed him on the forehead and stroked his hair.

Dr. Carrington checked the data on the machines and placed a stethoscope against Brandon's chest. His heart was racing, but not dangerously so and his breathing was ragged. A peculiar odor was coming from his mouth. Part of the scent smelled like sea water, but under normal circumstances, that would not be possible, he thought.

Brandon's eyes opened and he stared at everyone in the room. "Where am I and who are all you people?" He tried to move, and then he saw the restraints holding him tightly to the bed. "Why am I restrained? I need to get back up on deck before the Japs hit us again."

The sedative had begun to work and before Brandon could utter another word, he was out like a light.

The doctor noticed the confusion on the faces of the rest of the staff. He closed the door and said, "What you have just heard will not be repeated to anyone outside of this room. Should I find out that others have learned what has occurred here, there will be severe consequences." He went on to tell them that this case involved a paranormal possession of the patient by his grandfather. "There is a lot we need to find out about what is going on in this man's mind and body and the fewer people that know about it the better. I'm going to put him in a private room and keep him sedated until I can get a psychiatrist to see him. I also need to tell my superiors what I plan to do. Do any of you have a problem with this?"

When each person present told him no, he said, "Good. I'm concerned about Mr. Pederson's mental state and I am leaning toward the conclusion that he may also be possessed by the spirit of his grandfather. When a doctor with that expertise is able to question him, I am hoping we can come up with answers to many of the questions I have. You can all get back to work now and thank you for keeping this under wraps."

The staff left and a few minutes later two patient transporters came in to take Brandon up to a private room. JoAnne went with them as Russ called his boss.

Inside Brandon Pederson, Al, who had heard everything, was working on a plan. As soon as he awakened him, he would get out of this place.

6

Russ escorted JoAnne to his small office where he offered her a seat. After sitting down at his desk, he took a moment to get his thoughts together before speaking. She opened her mouth, but he put a finger up, silencing her before she even uttered a sound. "JoAnne, I'm afraid I don't know anything about what Brandon may be going through, and I honestly don't know if a psychiatrist would be helpful, but it probably couldn't hurt."

"He is scaring me, Russ. Listening to him speak, I noticed that it was not Brandon's voice, but since I never heard his grandfather speak, I don't know if it was him, either. I think only his wife, Eleanor, would know if Al was definitely possessing his grandson."

Russ rubbed his chin and nodded. "You could be right, because we are dealing with something that I've never come across, or for that fact, never even read about. Right now, I guess the best thing is for him to stay sedated and rest. I'm sure you are getting tired too."

"Yeah, I am a little whipped. I think I should probably call a cab to take me to the North Carolina and get our car. Then it will only take about a half hour to get back to Wrightsville."

"I could save you some time and drive you there and then you could get your car tomorrow."

She shook her head. "Thanks for the offer, but I'd rather get the car and drive back myself. That way if anything happens during the night, someone can call me and I'll come right back."

"Okay, but I insist upon driving you to the ship."

She smiled. "I accept."

A few minutes after they pulled out of the lot, Al awakened Brandon.

7

He got out of bed, being careful not to pull out his IV; that would come out soon enough. His clothing was in the small closet, but it was a little out of reach. Using all of Al's skills, Brandon managed to create a handle with a hook, using parts from the different machines in the room. Once built, he was able to grab the bag that held his personal items. He pulled it toward him and then quickly put on his socks and pants and then his shoes. He put his left arm through the sleeve of his shirt and then pulled the IV from his arm. He quickly opened the window, and then stepped into the small closet, closing the door behind him.

Moments later, a nurse stepped into the room, saw the empty bed and the open window and shouted out, "The patient has left the hospital though an open window."

He heard footsteps approaching the room and whomever it was rushed toward the window. "I don't see anyone out there," a male voice announced. "Call security and have them scour the grounds. If he's gone, our asses are gonna fry." Al heard the footsteps recede.

Quietly he stepped from the closet and turned toward the open door. Nobody was in sight, so he slowly stepped out from the door. His plan worked; everyone was searching for him after he basically hid in plain sight.

He walked past the elevator and found the stairs. Taking them two at a time, feeling exhilarated, Al went up instead of down. He stepped out into a corridor and soon found what he wanted. A cart full of scrubs was against the wall. He grabbed a set and threw them over his uniform. Once disguised as a hospital employee, he found a clipboard and scanned the papers, as though he was working on a case. Inside the nurse's station, he spotted a badge lying on one of the desks. He slipped it into his pocket and moved on, finding the staff locker room. He swiped the badge, stepped inside and found sweatpants and sneakers that were his size. He took off the scrubs and covered his Navy fatigues with the sweatpants. He found a light jacket to wear over his shirt. He also found a St. Louis Cardinals baseball cap, a pair of sunglasses and a backpack to complete his disguise. He clipped the badge to his jacket with the back of the badge facing outward and strolled from the locker room, past the nurses' station, down the elevator and out the front door, seeing security guards searching for him. He nodded to one and waved, getting a wave in return. Moments later he was walking a street in Wilmington, ready to put his plan to work.

8

Russ and JoAnne had arrived the parking lot of the North Carolina Battleship Museum and she had opened the passenger door when his cell rang.

"Doctor Carrington speaking."

He listened for a while and then turned to JoAnne. "Brandon escaped from the hospital."

"How is that possible, Doctor Carrington?"

Russ was taken aback that she didn't question him informally. He shook his head. "Apparently he opened a window and got out that way…Yes, I'm still here." He listened for a minute and then hit off and put his phone in his pocket. "Somehow he must have hidden somewhere because ten minutes or so after he supposedly left through the window, a badge was reported missing. I guess he stayed in the hospital, took that badge and probably used it to get into a locker room and disguise himself. He probably walked right out through the front door."

"Al must have done this all because I don't think Brandon could have done it, although working as a nurse at the VA, he knows a lot about security."

"JoAnne, I am so sorry this happened. Do you think he would try to come back here?"

"If he'd have the car keys, he might…Shit! He has a spare key inside his wallet, so he could be on the way back, but unless he swam across the river, it would take him some time to get here."

"I'm going to call a friend of mine who's a cop in Wilmington. He's working right now.

9

Al was feeling more in control of Brandon with each passing minute. He stepped into a bar and walked to the bathroom. He took a piss, and as he washed his hands, he noticed that his features were replacing Brandon's. Soon he would be a young man in a totally different world and when he found the gold his life would be much better. The address he needed to go to was burned in his-Brandon's-memory.

He looked at the paper towel dispenser for several moments. After figuring out how to get some, by passing his hand over a sensor, he dried his hands and tossed the hospital badge in the trash can. He needed a beer and had to figure out how to use the cell phone so he could call a cab and get to the ship and his car. JoAnne may have gone there already but he couldn't be sure.

The bartender set bottle of Yuengling in front of him. He picked it up and took a long pull, smiling after he swallowed. Seventy years is much too long between beers, Al, he thought and then he laughed out loud, garnering the attention of a few patrons. He lifted his beer and saluted them, causing them to smile and turn back to their conversations or their loneliness.

He inquired where he could pick up a pack of cigarettes after he ordered another beer.

"You can get cigarettes at the Tobacco Store just down the street." The bartender answered as he picked up the empty bottle and tossed it into a trash can behind the bar.

Al noticed the shape of a cigarette package in his shirt and asked, "Can I bum one from you?" Looking around he also asked for an ashtray.

The bartender shook out a Pall Mall. Al took it and slipped it in his mouth.

"Sorry, buddy, this is a non-smoking bar, like most of the joints in the country."

Al gave him a quizzical look. "Non-smoking? You gotta be joking, right?"

"You been living under a rock, friend? Most places are non-smoking. However, you can take your smoke and your drink and go out back on the patio. Smoking is allowed there."

Al grabbed his bottle and walked out to the back patio. Two men and three women were out there smoking and when Al realized he didn't have matches or a lighter, sauntered over to the three women. He nodded. "Could I get a light from one of you pretty ladies?' He asked.

Two of them were a tad overweight, but not too bad while the third was an absolute knockout. She was the one who flicked a Bic and lit his smoke.

"Thanks, ma'am." He took a deep drag, inhaled and

coughed his fool head off. The women laughed and the men smirked.

Once he settled down he laughed too. "It's been a while since I had a butt. Guess it got to me."

One of the slightly overweight women said, "I know how that is. I tried to quit a couple of years ago. I didn't smoke for about three months and when I lit up again, same thing happened." She lit another one from the one she was smoking.

I wonder how you'd do if you've been dead for seventy years and then tried it again. Al wanted to tell her, and the others, aloud, but he didn't want to give his secret away.

They all smoked and drank for about an hour, Al replenishing their drinks a couple of times. Finally he said, "Well, I gotta catch a cab and head over to the battleship."

The good looking one, Serena was her name, said, "I can take you over, Al. It's not too far out of my way. My friends are headed in the opposite direction, so it would be no problem at all."

"Thanks, Serena, I do appreciate that."

"What do you do on the ship, Al?"

"Security. Gotta keep people from creating mischief."

"Maybe we'll see you sometime soon." The heaviest girl, Nona, stated, as she adjusted her bra, staring into his eyes, which had dropped to her breasts.

"Yeah, maybe you will. If I had some phone numbers it would be easier to get a hold of you."

She took a card from her purse. "This is my business number and I'll write my cell on the back."

The other woman, Brenda, did the same."

Serena didn't bother since he would soon be in her car.

10

As soon as he was comfortably seated, Serena leaned over and kissed him hard, rubbing his crotch.

He responded and fondled her left breast and felt a

stirring in his loins that he last felt just before he shipped out. His thoughts turned to Eleanor and he stopped, quickly pulling his hand back.

"Am I out of line, Al?" She asked as she smoothed her shirt.

"No, but I should have told you that I'm married." He felt Brandon trying to reclaim his body, but he really did feel that way.

She started the car and headed toward the bridge. She'd take him to the ship and then they could both get on with their lives.

"I am sorry, Al. Have you seen her lately?"

"No, it's been over 71 years. The ship was hit and we had to go back to Pearl Harbor for repairs. I knew we'd be there for awhile, so I had a friend send her a letter and a couple of days after we got there, Eleanor arrived and we were able to spend quite a bit of time with each other before I had to go back to war. It was such a fun time and…"

As he rambled on, Serena really became frightened. How could this man, who appeared to be in his mid-twenties, talk about a woman, who would be in her mid-nineties if she were still alive. She continued driving because she didn't want to set him off.

"…I hated to see it end. A little over nine months later, I received word that I was a father. My son was born on December 21st, 1943." He stopped talking and looked at her. "I'm scaring you, aren't I?"

Although she kept her composure, Serena nodded, not knowing if her voice would work.

Suddenly, Brandon pushed through. "Serena, listen carefully because I don't know how much time I will have. My name is Brandon Pederson. My wife, JoAnne, and I are staying at the Carolina Temple Island Inn in Wrightsville Beach. My grandfather, Al, possessed me earlier today when I stepped on the deck of the North Carolina. He was murdered during a battle in 1944. He knows where his killer lives and he is trying to get there to avenge his death." As he was talking he found a cash register receipt in his wallet and scribbled the address of the vacant lot the ghosts told him and JoAnne about yesterday. "Give this to the police as soon as possible because I don't want anyone to die." He placed his hand on top of hers.

A few moments later, Al was once again in control. He saw his hand on top of hers and squeezed hard. "What did my grandson tell you?"

"She told me who you were and that you have possessed him, but I don't understand any of this. You're hurting me, Al." She began to sob.

He let go of her hand. "Did he tell you anything else?"

She shook her head and Al believed her. "Just drop me off in the parking lot and then you can go."

They drove the rest of the way in silence and when he saw JoAnne and the doctor in the parking lot, he squeezed her hand again. "Keep going. There's someone by my car and I won't be able to get to it."

"Where do you want to go?"

He released her hand again. "Take me to the nearest bus station."

11

When JoAnne saw the car pass by on the road outside the parking lot, she wondered if it could be Brandon. It seemed to slow down slightly because she could pick up the sound of the engine noise which had momentarily grown softer just before the car drove off, turning on to Battleship Road NE. Brandon always kidded her about her acute hearing, but she was glad to have it. On more than one occasion, her hearing had got them out of potential danger on the highway, especially under foggy conditions. One time especially, when they were on the way home from a party, both of them having had a little too much to drink, Brandon stopped at a stop sign. He lowered both side windows and listened, hearing nothing, and he was ready to cross the intersection, when she heard the sound of an engine. She yelled stop and he hit the brakes, avoiding crashing into a casino bus by less than a foot.

"Russ, I think Brandon may be in the car that just passed by."

He hadn't noticed it but said, "Should we follow him?"

"No, I could be wrong. I still think he wants to come here and if I leave, I'll miss him."

"I could trail them and if it is him, I think I could convince him to come back with me and then back to the hospital. You have keys, so you could stay in the car and wait for me to come back."

"Okay, let's give that a try. If it's not him, give me a call and then you can head home and I'll go back to Wrightsville."

He hopped in his car and took off in the direction of a car he had not seen. What were the chances that he would find it? He drove down Battleship Road.

She turned on her phone, not realizing that it had been off all day. Moments after he left, it rang. "Russ, is there anything wrong?" She asked.

"Mrs. Pederson, this is Rick Conlen. Something happened last night that I need to tell you about."

Thursday, June 19th, 2014

Richard Conlen's Office, Southport, North Carolina

A ghost answered. "Mr. Conlen. My name is Justin Nonnemacher and I was a sailor on board the Battleship North Carolina in 1944. I know how Al Pederson died and after all these years, the five of us want to see justice done for a crime that was committed on that ship. Al did not fall overboard he was murdered." Hearing the sound of the door opening, the ghost stopped speaking.

Denise stepped inside and immediately saw the five ghosts. She began to shake and nearly screamed, but Rick calmed her down.

"Why are these ghosts in your office, Rick?"

"It's a long story and I'll tell you about it sometime, but right now I can tell you that I can see and communicate with the dead. I don't know why they want you to see them, but I'm guessing that it might be connected to the Pedersons. Perhaps you should sit down while I fill you in.

He told her why the ghosts had come to him but there was something he didn't understand. He looked them over again and asked, "Why are you all in the spirit world? I see that you are all of different ages, and since only one of you looks young enough to have died in the war, I'm trying to figure out what has kept you together in the afterdeath? I call it that because I figure that if you would have gone to heaven or hell, you can't walk in the afterlife.

Jim Richman, the youngest of the ghosts got up from the chair he was sitting in. "I was killed in November of 1944. We had just rode out Typhoon Cobra after joining up with the task force when we came back out from getting repairs done. We supported air strikes on Leyte, Luzon and the Visayas. After that the kamikazes hit us and that's when I got it. One little fucking piece of shrapnel hit me right in the heart and I was gone in seconds."

"So why do you think you haven't moved on into the

afterlife?"

He shrugged. "Maybe because I died violently, or maybe because I was one hell of a sinner in my short life. Just don't know, counselor. I'm hoping if we can help Al, maybe then we'll get our final reward, whatever it may be."

Leroy 'Pops' Hamilton chimed in. "I was a badass, I'm sorry to say. After the war, I went back home to the Bronx and I had a hell of a time to find a job. I had been a plumber, but couldn't find work because all the jobs were taken when we left for war. There was no way in hell I was going to take a job washing dishes or cleaning shithouses. I had just fought for my country and with all the guys coming back, most of them much smarter then me, good paying jobs were hard to find. A lot of guys went back to school on the GI bill to further their education, but I didn't want nothing to do with that."

"Why wouldn't you want to get an education since it was so cheap to go back to college on the GI bill?" Denise inquired, having become interested in this conversation with the dead.

"Well," he smiled, "because I was the old man and that's how I got the name Pops. I just didn't want to go back to school with all the former military guys way younger than me and I guess I regretted it. I got in with the wrong crowd. We did and sold drugs and booze. Needing money to support our habits, three of us decided to rob a bank one day. Long story short, the robbery went askew and I was gut shot by a cop. Lasted a week with intense pain until I died. I was only thirty-two."

Carl Mantle looked at the assemblage of spirits, and then looked at the clock on the wall. He said, "Looks like he's late, so since I actually lived longer than all of us here, I'll tell my story. I really had a good life after the war. Before the war, I was a pro boxer and never lost a fight, but I didn't want to go back into the ring. Guess I had enough fighting in the four years in the navy. I got a job at General Motors and worked there for thirty-five years making really good money. I got married two years after the navy, raised four kids in a nice home. Gail and I were able to send them to college and they are very successful. We had two grandkids and we were so happy until Gail was taken from me in '82. She was out for a walk with two neighbor women and was struck by a drunk driver. I had a hell of a time functioning after she was gone, and I started drinking heavily. Smoked more than ever, too. I had been a two pack a day smoker since I was about seventeen and once I was alone, I usually burned through three packs a day. About a year after Gail died, I was drinking a beer and having a smoke. Neither tasted very good, so I dumped about a half a bottle down the sink and crushed out my butt. Never touched either after that day and turned my life around, spending more time with the grandkids and volunteering at the city hospital until the inevitable finally hit me. I had lung cancer and once I was diagnosed I only lasted for three months. It was a brutal way to die and I wouldn't wish it on anyone."

The front door opened and an old man stepped in. He saw the ghosts and smiled. Nodding his head he said, "Now I guess I know why I had to be here today." He looked at Rick and Denise. "I guess Al is going to show up sooner or later and he needs a live person to tell the law how he died and who killed him."

"Who are you?" Rick inquired.

The old man sat down in a comfortable leather chair and ran a hand through his thinning, white hair. "I'm Harmon Eckland and when I was on the North Carolina, I was petty officer in charge of the engine room. I was the man who exchanged gold coins for cash with Al, among others. The rate was 2 to 1 and I made a good amount of money this way. Looking back, had I not sold the gold coins, I would be worth a great deal of money, much more than I am worth now." He laughed, throwing his head back. Then he turned serious. "If Al's coins are ever found, the value of them would be about a half a million dollars."

Rick leaned forward and placed his elbows on his desk. The ghosts were getting a little fidgety and he wondered why. "How much gold did you exchange during the war?"

He took a cigar from his jacket and snipped the end before placing it in his mouth. He knew he couldn't smoke, but he just liked the taste of the tobacco on his tongue. "I traded about forty-thousand dollars in gold for about eighty-five grand. I got lucky after the war and made some good investments. My net worth is over five million dollars right now."

"That's a lot of money. Do you have a family?" Denise became very interested in the conversation, but she still didn't know what her role in all this was going to be.

"Yes, miss. My wife and I will be married sixty-eight years next month and we have two kids; a boy and a girl, seven grandchildren and three great grandchildren. They will all be very well taken care of when Maggie and I are gone."

Rick was typing on his laptop and he stopped to ask a question. "I can see why someone would want to kill Mr. Pederson and take his money, but who masterminded his death.

The ghost of Jeff Ambrose said, I'll take that one. "Al Pederson was a terrific poker player and he took the five of us for thousands of dollars while we were aboard ship. I know I was really pissed off and wanted to get my money back." He told them about following Al and finding out where the gold was hidden. "After I found out where he put his gold, I told 'Pops'. We decided that we'd kill Al and steal his gold, but the war got in the way and we didn't get the chance."

"So the two of you were willing to commit murder for money? How much are we talking about?" Rick inquired.

"Over the time we were out to sea he took us and a lot of other sailors for about fifteen grand."

"You all must have had a lot of money back in those

days to lose that much."

"Yeah, well, we all played poker with a lot of sailors whenever we had time. Most time on a ship is spent performing normal duties and there was quite a bit of downtime, unless we were involved in a battle. I know I won a couple of grand from sailors in other parts of the ship, but I lost most of it to Al. It was uncanny how he won so often." Carl Mantle offered.

"How many sailors were on board the ship during the war?" Rick asked.

Pops pointed to Jim Richman. "Ask him. He was like a fuckin' walking encyclopedia. The guy knows everything."

Jim smiled. He had moved and was sitting at Rick's desk, playing around on the laptop. "Man, I wish we would have had these all those years ago. It would take forever to find information in a library." He sighed and cold air drifted across Rick and Denise, causing them both to shake. "Anyway, there were over twenty-three hundred sailors on that ship, and a lot of us played poker or dice. Serving on a ship is probably ninety-five percent boredom once you have completed your daily duties, so there was a lot of free time. I didn't play as much as these guys, but I probably lost a couple of hundred to Al and I wanted to win my money back. He died before I had another chance to beat him."

"So which of you guys killed him?" Rick asked.

All of them shook their heads.

"Do any of you know who did it?"

Justin glided over to Denise and laid his hands on her shoulders, causing he to shiver. "You're not going to like this, but the murderer is your great uncle, Larry." He looked up at Rick. "Larry Scott is Al Pederson's killer.

Denise swooned, nearly fainting, but she got herself back together quickly.

"I knew he had been in the service, but I didn't know he was on the North Carolina. He's out of town and won't be back until the day after tomorrow, but I have a key to his house and we could go there tomorrow and check it out. I imagine you'll need to get a warrant."

Rick excused himself and stepped into another room. He punched in some numbers on his cell phone and when the other party answered they talked for several minutes. After he hung up, he stepped back out into his office and sat down. "We'll have a warrant tomorrow morning."

Friday, June 20th, 2014

Southport, North Carolina
Wilkes Barre, Pennsylvania
Kashima, Japan

1

Rick Conlen felt the warmth of the sun on his cheek and it woke him up. He turned on his side and kissed Denise. Her breathing told him that she was still in lala land. Figuring she would want to sleep a little bit longer, he slid out of bed and walked to the kitchen to make coffee. He opened the lid, put a filter in and added eight scoops of coffee. He took the carafe and filled it to the top, judging it with a finger. He poured the water in the coffeemaker, then closed the lid. He turned it on and heard the pitter-patter of dainty feet on the linoleum floor.

Denise came up behind him and slapped his bare ass and then she turned him around and kissed him, squeezing his penis and rubbing her leg against his.

He responded almost immediately, lifting her onto the kitchen table, making love as the scent of freshly brewing coffee spurred them on.

After, they sat down and savored the coffee, wolfing down a couple of sticky buns as well.

He said, "You know that if the police believe Harmon's story, your great uncle could go the prison for the rest of his life."

"I know, but if he killed Al Pederson, he has to pay for his crime."

"It's hard to fathom that someone could keep a murder secret for seventy years. Especially someone as prominent as Larry Scott. He's been an upstanding member of this community since he came back from the war."

"I remember my Great Aunt Lorraine telling us that Uncle Larry came back to Southport, basically flat broke and he got a job delivering milk. Several years later, he opened an ice cream shop and it was a very good business for him. With his savings he bought a garage and he had great mechanics working for him. As time passed, he bought some land and as Southport grew, he was able to sell the land and make a very good profit. In 1976 Uncle Larry paid for the entire rebuilding of The Holy Church of the Redeemer, where he had been a member since he was a little boy…"

Rick interrupted her. "Even back then that must have cost a tremendous amount of money and I can't see how he could have saved that much from what you have told me so far."

"You're right. He used to go to flea markets a lot to see what he could buy cheap and sell for a good profit. He bought a bunch of paintings one time and he thought he had found a rare painting by van Gogh. He had it appraised and sold it for over 78 million dollars. He wanted to do something important because he was always a devout man. Lorraine told me that in the war they nicknamed him Preacher because he was always reading the Bible. He has also helped so many unfortunate people by paying off mortgages, donating food, taking care of hospital bills and given cancer stricken kids free trips to Disney World. He also gave a large sum of money to the hospital and paid for an addition that would be reserved for him if and when he ever needed hospitalization."

"Why would he have committed murder, Denise? It just doesn't make sense with everything you have told me."

"I don't know. War does things to people I suspect, but killing a fellow sailor just doesn't fit with all I know about him."

Rick shrugged his shoulders. "We'll have to see what happens when we get an opportunity to talk to him. I'm going to try to get Brandon or JoAnne on the phone again. I haven't had any success since the ghost visits last night."

Both numbers took him to voice mail.

2

In Wilkes Barre, Pennsylvania, Eleanor Pederson awakened early. On June 20th of every year she just could not stay asleep. She went downstairs and filled the ancient aluminum coffee pot with water and then added five scoops of coffee into the aluminum basket. She placed the pot on a gas burner and turned up the heat. Although Brandon and JoAnne had given her a new coffeemaker five or six years ago, she still preferred to use the old pot. "Coffee tastes better in this pot than when it perks into one of those glass carafes," she used to tell her grandson and his wife.

As the coffee brewed, starting to fill the small kitchen with a wonderful scent, she put two slices of wheat bread into the toaster and took the butter dish from the refrigerator. She found a jar of strawberry jam on the back of a lower shelf and she was going to use it until she noticed fur growing on top of the jam. She tossed the bottle into a small plastic bucket that already contained an empty plastic milk container, a Sprite bottle, an empty butter tub and a bunch of plastic ware. Eleanor did not like to do dishes too often, so she used recyclables as often as possible.

The coffee pot started to whistle, steam coming from the spout, just as the toasted bread popped up. She poured a cup and took the bread to the table, spreading a light coat of butter on each slice. She added a teaspoon of creamer and a packet of Splenda into the coffee and stirred it slowly, watching the creamer turn the black coffee to a light brown.

Eleanor took a great deal of time eating her toast and drinking her coffee as she read the Times Leader newspaper.

When she started reading the obituaries, her hands

began to shake. The obituary of her husband, first ran in that newspaper on June 26th, 1944. She started reading it again, for the first time after seventy years.

On June 20th, Seaman Second Class Alfred Pederson was lost at sea and presumed dead. Pederson was serving as a gunners mate on the battleship North Carolina, engaged in a naval/air battle with Japanese forces west of the Marianas Island chain. How Pederson was lost is not known at this time, but it is possible he could have fallen overboard. He was 26 years old and at the time of his death he left a wife, Eleanor and a year old son, Alfred Junior. A Mass in his honor will be held at St. Mark's Episcopal Church in Plains on Sunday at 11 PM. Pederson attended church there from the age of ten until he entered the Navy in 1942.

Eleanor put the paper on the table and dried the tears running down her cheeks with her napkin. She sighed and picked up the paper again. The obituary was no longer there and she feared she was beginning to lose her mind. She suddenly felt faint and passed out in her chair.

3

Thirty-one year old billionaire industrialist Yoshiro Nagata took his iPhone from his inside jacket pocket and punched in the number. It was 9 AM in the time zone he was calling and he figured this would not be too early to call. As the dialed number rang, he thought back to the events that led to this call.

4

Last month, he was in a meeting, attempting to obtain yet another petrochemical company. One more would give him control of both the import and export business. The transaction would cost him upwards of sixty million American dollars, but he would see a tenfold return on his investment in less than four years.

"Gentlemen," he said, standing near the floor to ceiling window of his twenty-third floor office. "I know you will eventually give in and accept my offer, but I am prepared to sweeten the pot and include one hundred thousand shares of NagataChemCorp. That will give you a total of fifty-two million. You know the shares will increase in value in the not too distant future. My estimate is that you will earn six to eight million this year alone." He sat down in his desk chair and folded his hands in his lap. "Take all the time you need, as long as you can give me an answer within a week."

After the four men left, he stood up, walked to the bookcase and pressed a button revealing a hidden safe. He opened it and took out two hundred thousand dollars, planning to participate in a high stakes poker game. His work was pretty much finished for this day and he was preparing to leave when the door opened. Chiyo Nagana, his twenty-three year secretary burst inside, smiling from ear to ear.

"Yoshiro, I just received an email from the ship. Your grandfather's plane has been discovered at the bottom of the ocean and preparations are being made to raise it."

He smiled. "Thank you, Chiyo. I have been waiting for this day for such a long time. I'd like to do a video chat if you will set that up for me."

"Hai. I will have that ready to go in a few minutes." She turned on her heel and returned to her desk.

He sat down again, digesting this information. He had been searching for his grandfather's plane for nine years, wanting to put it on display in a park he was going to build to honor the pilots who lost their lives in the battle of the Marianas. His grandfather, Lieutenant Hiro Nagata, piloted a torpedo plane that disappeared during the battle. No one saw it get hit, but one pilot saw the small bomber dive into the sea. The family never received any more information and for years it had disturbed Yoshiro to the point where he couldn't sleep at night. He kept seeing ghostly images of his grandfather. When he became wealthy, he purchased a ship and the best submersible money could buy to find the wreck. If there was a wreck indeed, he always believed it would be found. Soon he would see it through a video link.

Chiyo buzzed him on the intercom. "Sir, I have a video link for you. Please reveal your screen."

Yoshiro pressed a button and the pocket wall opened revealing a sixty inch monitor. He saw Captain Daisuke Fuchida. "Daisuke, it is so good to see you. So you have found the plane."

"Yes, sir. It is your grandfather's plane. It is completely encased in some kind of crystal-like substance, and it is in pristine condition. I'm going to transfer you to the submersible so you can see it for yourself."

A moment later, Yoshiro was staring at the plane and he too was amazed at its condition. "Daisuke, this is remarkable. When it is returned to Kashima, I don't think it will take very long to get it back into near perfect condition. Once we end our conversation, I am going to immediately contact the contractors working on the memorial park to have them make ready the pedestal. This is so exciting."

"Yoshiro, there is something else we found that defies explanation. You're going to see something even more impossible than a seventy year old airplane preserved in this manner."

"What is it?"

"It's not an it, sir. It's a human being; an American military man, nearly perfectly preserved, encased in this crystal substance on the other side of the plane. I have no idea how or why this happened, but we're going to bring him up too. Some family will be pleasantly stunned to have their loved one returned."

The camera turned and Yoshiro was looking at the body encased in the crystal along with the airplane. The body was in beautiful condition although it appeared as though the man's neck had been snapped. His tongue was lying across his lips and his eyes were wide open. His hands were in a gripping position as though he wanted to latch on to something. Even the tattoo on his right arm was readable. Yoshiro smiled. The tattoo was an ace of spades and above the drawing of the highest playing card was a name. The man encased in crystal is Al Pederson. Finding family members should be very easy now.

"Sir, we have also discovered that the ship is German because there is a swastika painted on the side. The plane apparently hit it and when it did, the crystallization process began. Part of the ship's number is also visible and we are searching computer records to see if we can find out the name, and what it was doing in this part of the world."

"The Germans had some marvelous scientists; perhaps they were transporting something to Japan that would help them in the war effort. I look forward to what you find out."

"Soon as I get something, Yashiro, I will certainly contact you again. Talk to you soon, my friend."

"You too. I hope to find family members of Al Pederson soon, as well."

Sunday, November 14th, 1943

Near The Marianas Islands

Captain Siegfried Vogler stood on the deck of the ship, smoking a cigarette and drinking a brandy. The trip from Germany thus far had been uneventful and in two days he and his crew of seventeen would reach their destination. He looked toward the stern and stared at the canvas covering forty-two aluminum canisters containing a chemical compound discovered by two Jewish scientists in 1937. The scientists were forced to work for the German high command; the compound was going to be employed to encase many important German and Japanese people, insuring that both empires would be able to rebuild at a later time, if the war was lost.

His uncle was involved in the production of the compound, given the project number, K-306S97. It had taken these men nearly five years to find the catalyst that would make the substance work. Once the compound in these containers was introduced to salt water, a crystal like coating could be applied to a human body, preserving it until that time would come that the body could be resurrected, a living person again, capable of continuing on with the mission. The mission was to bury America and its allies, guaranteeing world domination for the Reich and the Empire of Japan.

The containers were to remain topside in the event the ship would be torpedoed. By not being in the hold they stood a better chance of surviving if the ship was sunk. If the containers were compromised, and salt water was introduced, the compound would just expand and cover everything it touched, rendering it useless, even if found in the future.

His first officer, Johan Kessler, strode up to him. He saluted and said, "Sir, there are a few problems I need to report."

Vogler returned his salute. "Why didn't you use the intercom instead of coming out here?"

"That is one of the problems. The radio does not work and all the electrical functions of the ship have ceased to operate. The engine has died and we have no power of any kind."

"Strange that I didn't feel us stop," he replied.

"That's the thing, Captain. We haven't stopped. Something is pulling us forward."

"Does anyone have any idea what is causing all this?"

Before he received a reply, the moon slipped behind a cloud, eliminating all light. In the darkness, Vogler felt the ship shudder and begin to slip down into the water. He had no idea what was causing his ship to be physically pulled under the water, but in moments, it was gone.

He and six of his crew managed to swim away from the pull, but they knew they would not be able to survive in the water very long. Three of his men were screaming in the blackness and he could hear flesh being torn and bones breaking as they were being eaten alive by sharks that almost always followed ships. They fed on the uneaten food being tossed overboard after every meal.

Less than ten minutes later, his screams mixed with the rest until the stillness was restored.

The ship and its precious cargo would rest at the bottom of the ocean until a Japanese plane would find its way to the deck, destroying many of the containers that would spill the contents into the ocean, encasing the plane and the dead pilot.

Friday, June 20th, 2014

Wilkes Barre, Pennsylvania
Kashima, Japan
Wilmington and Wrightsville Beach, North Carolina

1

After fourteen rings and not being sent to voice mail, Yoshiro hung up. He understood that many people in that age bracket did not have computers, cell phones, or even voice mail on their land lines. He would try again later but he took some time and asked Chiyo if she could find any of her relatives using social media and The White Pages. She agreed and when he ended that conversation, he realized just how important she was to him, not only as a secretary, but as a confidant. He was going to give her a special gift for all her hard work.

2

When she finally opened her eyes, Eleanor knew she had to go to Wrightsville Beach and meet up with JoAnne. She looked at the clock on the wall and saw it was 6:10. She had only passed out for a minute or two. She felt as though Al had been found, although she realized that possibility was way off the charts. His body was at the bottom of a violent ocean and the chance that even bones could have survived was not even remotely probable…yet, she couldn't shake the feeling.

She picked up the phone and dialed the airport. She was able to book a flight that would leave at 10:19 and arrive in Wilmington at 3:02 PM. From there she would take a cab to the Carolina Temple Island Inn and stay in Brandon and JoAnne's room. She got up from the table and went into her bedroom to pack. Although she was deathly afraid of flying, if she didn't do this, she would never forgive herself.

At 8:47 she stepped outside to the waiting cab and headed to the airport, missing the call that was to come minutes later.

3

In her cubicle, just outside of her boss's office, Chiyo began her search on Facebook. She typed in Pederson and found over a hundred pages with that name. She merely clicked on each link and pasted the prepared letter knowing it might take a long time to get any kind of response. Midway through her search, she received a hit. She clicked on the notification and found out that Al Pederson had a grandson named Brandon, who lived in Wilkes Barre, Pennsylvania.

Using an iPad, she found his name and number on The White Pages and called it. She was actually surprised to see that someone in his thirties had a land line. She was sent to voicemail and heard a female voice say, "Hi, you've reached Brandon and JoAnne. We can't come to the phone right now, but you can reach us on our cell phones. His is 570-555-0379 and I am 0378. Have a great day.

She stood up, smoothing her skirt and checking her hair before she knocked on Yashiro's door. He summoned her inside where he was seated at his desk, berating someone, probably via Skype. His skin had reddened and he was louder and more demonstrative than she had ever seen him in the past. He motioned for her to take a seat and when she did so, her skirt rose to the middle of her thighs, making him smile even as he continued his tirade.

4

Eleanor checked her bag and had time to go the Wings Restaurant and Bar to have a cup of coffee and a muffin, not having time to eat after everything that had gone on earlier. After finishing, she went to Northeast PA News and Gifts to buy a book for the flight. She found a new mystery novel, picked it up and strolled to the counter deciding to get some candy to munch on as well.

She sat down on a hard plastic chair, sipped coffee and started to read her book before her flight was announced. Her apprehension for flying was beginning to make her sweat and she came so close to changing her mind and going back home. She couldn't do that of course, because the mystery surrounding Al's death needed to be solved and she was sure it would be unraveled in North Carolina.

5

Yashiro, still naked, watched Chiyo dress. She leaned forward as she stepped into her panties so he could take a good look at her breasts. Slowly, she pulled the silky, blue bikini briefs over her legs, stopping long enough to allow him one more look at the tuft of hair that he loved to run his tongue over. She finally pulled her panties all the way up and she saw he was hard again.

He motioned her to come to him and she lowered herself on to her knees, beginning to lick and suck him furiously until he came in her mouth. She swallowed and then stood up to finish dressing.

After she dressed, he watched her walk into his private bathroom to fill a basin with soapy water. She came back out, kneeled again and gently washed and dried his genitals, looking into his eyes and smiling all the while. When she finished, she took the basin back to the bathroom, then came over to the couch and sat down.

"How is the plane to be raised from the ocean? After seeing the photos, I consider that the mission was successful only because the ship was resting on that shelf, less than a thousand feet down." She inquired, stroking his cheek.

"I have been informed that the captain of the

submersible is attempting to cut the plane free from the partially encased ship with a laser and though it is tedious work, the plane and the American sailor should be freed within a few days. They will bring them to the surface slowly, because they don't know if the crystal like material will decompose once it is outside of the saltwater environment it is now in." He stroked her face and kissed her. He was finished with talk and wanted more sex.

After they made love again, he invited her into his shower, which he had only done once before. When they were both dressed again, he went back to his desk and she back to hers. The business of making money never ended and Yashiro had his eyes set on becoming the wealthiest man in the world. Before closing the door, she watched him work, typing on his laptop and talking into his blue tooth. She hoped he would have room in his life for her, because she had fallen in love with him. She closed the door and went back to her work.

6

An hour after arriving in Wilmington, Eleanor strolled into the Carolina Temple Island Inn and was met by Mary Wright.

"May I help you, ma'am," Mary inquired.

"Yes, I am Eleanor Pederson. My grandson Brandon and his wife JoAnne are staying here and I was wondering if I would be able to stay in their room with them until they leave."

"You could, Mrs. Pederson, but they only have a queen bed and the room is rather small. I can, however, give you an open room until Sunday morning. After that we are booked solid for the rest of the summer. Would that be okay with you?"

She nodded. "That would be fine."

As Mary took her information, Eleanor asked, "Do you know where Brandon and JoAnne are today. I haven't been able to reach either one and I'm a little concerned. In my experience, they never have their cell phones turned off. Young people have so many conveniences today, don't you think?"

"Yes, they do. Today's technology has made our jobs so much easier, information can be gathered so quickly that sometimes it makes my head spin. I enjoy today's phones. I can talk to, text with, or use video to contact my kids and grandkids. My husband, Steve literally lives on his phone during rental season. I know they were going to go into Wilmington today to visit the battleship North Carolina, but I don't know when they left or when they are returning."

Eleanor nodded. "That was my husband's ship. He was lost at sea seventy years ago today, but this morning I had the strangest experience."

"Would you like to talk about it? We could sit out on the back porch and I could pour us some iced tea."

"Yes, that would be lovely. After that, I think I am going to lie down and rest. Flying down here took a lot out of this old woman."

Friday, June 20th, 2014

Battleship North Carolina Parking Lot
Southport, North Carolina
Wrightsville Beach, North Carolina
Wilmington, North Carolina

1

"What happened last night, Rick?"

"I was visited by ghosts from Al's ship and the man who traded the gold to him. Harmon Eckland was a petty officer who worked in the engine room and he is now 96 but Denise told me he really looks fantastic for his age. He knows Larry Sanders killed Al and we are going to Sanders' house tomorrow with a search warrant. Hopefully all this will be over in a short time so you and Brandon will be able to return to your lives."

"That is wonderful news. Why aren't you going to his house today?"

"He's out of town until either late tonight or mid-morning tomorrow. He is a philanthropist and has given away large sums of money to charity and to rebuild a church here in the town. I think a lot of people are going to be shocked to find out that he murdered a fellow sailor. This news is going to be very hard for the people of Southport to accept, considering his stature in the community. Hell, they even named a wing after him at the hospital because he donated so much money."

"Is there a possibility he could get away with murdering Al? There is no body and only the word of one person, a person who did illegal things in the service."

"Anything is possible, but at least I'll get an opportunity to question him and try to find out what he knows. I'm sure that he'll be able to retain a high caliber attorney, but I want a shot at him, JoAnne."

"Well, I have news for you." She told him what had

95

occurred today and what was going on at this moment. "Russ took off after the car I think Brandon was in, but I haven't heard from him yet. Rick, I don't know what he's going to do because he's not himself anymore."

"Let me know when you find him because we need to get him off the street where we can watch him and keep him out of serious trouble. I have some work to do here and Denise is going to help me find out more information about the men who served with Al. I expect they will return sometime soon."

"Thanks for telling me what is going on there and I'll get back to you soon, I hope."

"Yeah, take care, JoAnne."

She decided to check her messages and was surprised when she saw Eleanor had called several times but there was also a message from a Chiyo Nagana in Japan.

2

Chiyo had just stepped out from the shower when she heard the phone ring. She reached for it, dripping water on the screen. "Hello, this is Chiyo."

"Ms. Nagana, this is JoAnne Pederson and I'm returning your call, although I don't know you and I don't know anyone in Japan. What do you want of me?"

Chiyo listened carefully, detecting a little edginess in the American woman's voice when she asked the question. Other than that, she sounded pleasant enough. "I was hoping to speak to your husband. Is he nearby?"

"No, I'm sorry. He is out of touch at the moment. Again, I must ask, what do you want of me?"

"It's a long story that goes back to a German ship that was lost in 1943 and continues with its recent discovery. I would like to talk to both of you in detail at some point, but for now, let me just say that the body of your husband's grandfather, Al, has been found about a thousand feet under water near the Marianas Island." She paused to let this information sink in and to see if Mrs. Pederson would comment without hearing more.

"How could you possibly know that it is Al? After seventy years under water, there can't be much left of him, if anything."

"Chiyo sat down on the toilet; she had to pee, but she didn't want the conversation put on hold until she finished. "Under normal circumstances, that would be true, but your husband's grandfather was found encased in some kind of crystal-like substance and even after all these years, Al Pederson's body is in pristine condition."

Now it was JoAnne's turn to sit. "Ms. Nagana, I find this information preposterous and somehow I think you must be mistaken…"

"Please call me Chiyo. I'm going to send you a picture so you can see for yourself." As she pulled up the photo and sent it to JoAnne's phone she continued. "My boss, Yashiro Nagata, is one of the wealthiest men in the world. For many years, he has been searching for his grandfather's airplane, which disappeared under mysterious circumstances. When the plane went down, it disturbed some containers lashed to the German ship and the liquid in the containers when infused with salt water turned into this crystal-like substance. Yoshiro's grandfather's plane was coated with the substance, preserving it and his grandfather as well. Apparently, a short time later, Al Pederson's body was encased in the substance too."

JoAnne had received the picture, actually several pictures and although she never saw Al Pederson in the flesh, the body bore a remarkable resemblance to pictures of him. She saw his neck was cocked in such an angle that it could have been snapped and his hands appeared as though he had been trying to grab something. She didn't understand why she was having so much trouble believing this since she and Brandon had been seeing ghosts. "Chiyo, these are amazing pictures. Have the plane and

Al's body been brought to the surface?"

"Not yet. Hopefully within a day or two, they should be here in Japan. Yoshiro is very anxious to see the plane and the bodies and once he understands what happened, he's going to inform the media and the world will know of this discovery at that time. Could you and your husband come to Japan next week to see all this in person?"

"I can't answer that right now, but I am going to tell you what is going on with my husband."

Ten minutes later, Chiyo replied. "I am so sorry, JoAnne. It's good that you will be able to confront the murderer, and having the pictures I sent you will certainly be evidence of foul play in Al's demise. I am leaving for the office soon and I'll have Yashiro contact you at that time."

"Thanks. I appreciate it. All I know is that I want this all to end and get my husband back."

3

Al Pederson, who had taken over Brandon Pederson's body, got off the bus and started to walk. He wanted to get to Larry Scott's house before the attorney figured out that Scott was the man who killed Al. Al figured that if he finished his old navy buddy off, he'd finally be able to leave his grandson's body and receive his final reward, whatever it may be. He didn't know if his gambling, drinking, and smoking qualified him as a died-in-the-wool, card carrying sinner, but whatever was to come, after 70 years in limbo, he was ready. Having his grandson kill Scott would not bode well with his standing in the church, but the man needed killing for what he had done.

He stood across the street and cased Scott's property. He didn't see a car and there was no garage, so he pretty much figured that his old shipmate was not at home. Not having any idea how long Larry would be gone, Al was trying to figure out what he should do. He could hang out here, simply by waiting where he was at, without sequestering himself deeper in the property. He found a space just to the left of the two car garage where he could sit down and the small shrubs would act as a blind, allowing him to see out, but nobody could see him. The house was vacant, a for sale sign in the front yard, so Al was pretty sure no one would pull in unless the realtor would be showing the home today. He didn't know how long he would have to hunker down here, but he was willing to stay for whatever amount of time it took.

He sat down in the four inch high grass and lit up a cigarette. After learning that more and more people were quitting the habit, he began to cut down, not wanting to get Brandon hooked on the habit once he decided to leave his body. He smoked slowly, savoring each drag, drawing it deep into his lungs and holding it for a good long time before blowing the smoke through pursed lips. He wished he had a beer or a coffee to go with it, but you can't always have what you want, he mused.

After watching the house for nearly an hour, he fell asleep sitting up. After awakening, he stood up, stretched and found a place to urinate. He walked back to his hiding place, laid down in the grass and began to snore, the dream of his last day alive tingling all his nerve endings, causing his body to twitch uncontrollably.

4

Al stood at the railing of the ship, staring out into the darkness. In the distance he could see tracers flying through the air toward the water. Some Jap plane was probably firing at one of the ships in the large task force. He was glad that they weren't shooting at the North Carolina because he was truly getting fed up with the constant fear of his ship being sunk and he would be lost forever in this large expanse of water; his body would probably never be found.

The last two days were pretty brutal, mostly for the enemy, but every American life lost could never be replaced. He so wanted to get home and see Eleanor and his son.

As he lit up a cigarette, a hand touched his shoulder.

"Nice night, Al. Do you think we'll see more action soon?"

"Don't know, Preacher. Maybe we're done for now, but the closer we get to Japan, the hairier it's likely to get." He took another drag. "Couldn't you sleep either?"

Larry shook his head. "No. It's hard to get to sleep sometimes. I turned on my flashlight and started reading my Bible and after about ten minutes of reading, I noticed you weren't in your bunk. How long have you been out here?"

"About an hour, I guess. I like the darkness. It's so peaceful, but I'm really getting homesick to see my wife and son. Seems like forever since I've been home." He took a long drag of the cigarette and flipped it over the railing, watching it burn out as it traveled toward the water. "I'm always amazed how long you can see the redness of the butt after you toss it. It gets black as hell out here."

"Yeah, me too. I like being on the water, but I would rather be on a boat fishing. That's why I love Southport. Fishing off the coast is usually very rewarding. We'll never go hungry anyway."

"I never was much of a fisherman, but I still enjoy hunting. Getting a buck in your sight and firing a kill shot just feels so good. After I get home from this war, though, I wonder if I will want to hunt again. I'm tired of all the killing, even though we never see the faces of the Japs we shoot down."

"Are you going back to your old job when you get home, Al?"

"Don't know that either. I've done pretty well playing cards so maybe I'll open a garage. I always did like to work on cars, so I might as well make some money doing it. What about you, Larry? He lit up two cigarettes and passed one to him.

"Well, Al. I have been thinking about that for a long time and praying for a sign to do what I feel I have to do. I want to go to The Wilmington School of Theology and become a pastor, but I don't know how I'll come up with the money?"

"How much is it a year?"

"Four years will cost several thousand, and I don't have it?"

"So what is this sign you are looking for and how is it going to help you get the money?"

Just as Larry was ready to answer, a shooting star passed through the night sky. He smiled and said, "I just saw a shooting star and I believe that is my sign. I know you have a lot of gold stashed and I know where it is. It just isn't right to keep that money to build a garage, when I could use it for school and save many souls for the rest of my life."

Al was trying to comprehend the fact that his friend was going to probably kill him and take his gold. He was ready to react to whatever Larry was going to do, but he didn't know that Larry was so fast. After Larry hit him with something metallic, he felt hands around his neck, twisting and turning and then he felt his feet go out from under him as his neck was snapped. He tried to grab hold of a railing as he felt his body being shoved overboard.

5

He woke up, remembering how dying had felt and that when his nearly dead body hit the cold water, he almost screamed. It was over so quickly that he didn't get much time to realize what was happening to him underwater, but some of it was beginning to come back.

Through eyes wide with fright, he saw an airplane, actually a Jap fighter, encased in some kind of crystal-like substance. The closer he dropped toward the plane, the crystal-like substance started reaching up toward him and at the moment he truly died, he could feel the substance enveloping his body. It was not a bad sensation and he smiled, certain that his body was going to be preserved and found someday. He only hoped Eleanor was alive when this occurred so she would have some peace of mind and have remains to finally bury.

He looked toward the house again as the sun began to set. Larry's car was still not around and he wondered if staying in this yard would be a good idea. Brandon had a couple of hundred in cash and a couple of credit cards, so staying overnight in comfort would be no problem. He pulled out Brandon's cell phone and punched in 411 to get the number of a cab company.

6

Earlier, JoAnne arrived back at the Inn and found her grandmother-in-law sleeping on the bed. She nudged her and said, "Gamma, I'm back."

Eleanor awakened and turned toward her. She sat up and smiled. "It's so good to see you JoAnne. Is Brandon here?" She looked around and didn't see him.

JoAnne pulled a chair out from the small table that was built during World War II. She sat down and said, "Gamma, I have an awful lot to tell you about what has happened so far." She told Eleanor about every strange occurrence since seeing the ghost in the room on the way down, to everything that Brandon had done. "He was taken to the bus station in Wilmington where he boarded a bus to Southport. I think he is going to try to kill Larry Scott."

Eleanor absorbed all she heard, believing every word. She nodded her head and then told her granddaughter-in-law about Al's obituary in the morning paper. "What do you think that means, JoAnne?"

JoAnne was hesitant about telling her that Al's body had been found and that soon it would be returned to Wilkes Barre for a proper burial. She looked at Eleanor for what seemed like long minutes, but was only long seconds. She told her about the call she received from Japan and after telling her everything, waiting for a reaction, Eleanor just pursed her lips and looked toward the ceiling, tears forming in her eyes.

"I never had any hope that his body would be found, yet after reading his obituary again, I thought that Al was found, and I was being given a sign."

JoAnne stood up and then sat down beside her. "Would you like to see a picture of Gramps?"

Eleanor smiled and nodded. JoAnne scrolled to his

picture on her phone and showed it to her.

Eleanor clutched the phone to her chest and began to cry tears of joy. "It is amazing how well preserved his body is. Will they be able to remove him from the stuff he's encased in?"

"That I don't know but Al's body will be brought to the surface within the next couple of days. Only time will tell"

They embraced, hoping to get Al's body back and exorcising his spirit from Brandon.

"Gamma, tomorrow we are going to Southport."

7

Larry Scott left the Coin Market in Wilmington. He got an estimate on the value of the $7000 worth of gold coins he stole from Al's stash after he snapped his neck and tossed his body overboard. For seventy years he had been wrestling with what he had done and ever since he found out he only had a short time to live, he wanted to make financial restitution to Al's widow, Eleanor.

He remembered that night quite clearly. When he saw that shooting star, he was positive it was a sign from God for him to end Al's life. The man had taken so much money from his shipmates in poker games and even though he was never caught cheating, Larry was sure he could not be winning all this money without doing something illegal.

Over the years, he prayed often, hoping God would give him another sign. He wanted to give Eleanor Pederson the gold and confess to his crime, but one never came. After the last doctor appointment two weeks ago, he took the bad news pretty well. He felt that he had accomplished so much in his lifetime; helping the less fortunate have better lives. He nodded his head: he was ready to die, and he would suffer all the pain without any medication as part of his punishment.

Earlier he went to the great battleship for the first time since 1945. He actually got chills when he stepped on the deck, saluting the flag as he did every time he came back on board all those years ago. He walked around the deck, stopping at the quad 40 millimeter gun that he helped to load many times. The gun turret was chained off but when he told a volunteer that this was his gun and he'd like to sit at it one more time, the man acquiesced. Larry sat in the gun seat and put his hands on the wheel that turned the guns. It was inoperable, but the mere act of laying hands on it brought back so many memories. He thought he could even see some of the gun crew, but he was sure it was a hallucination.

He left the gun and walked down the metal stairs that led to the areas open to visitors below deck. He stepped into the galley, carefully lifting his legs one at a time to step over the bottom of the door. Seventy years ago, jumping over the threshold was a piece of cake, but his legs were not what they used to be, even only five or so years ago. He sat down at the table he used to eat at and again, he could have sworn he saw his gun mates. He rubbed his eyes and nobody was there. He didn't need to be seeing spirits of the dead; there was too much on his plate.

Larry found his sleeping area and could almost see Al and the others sitting on the floor playing cards, watching for any indication that Al was cheating. He could see himself in his bunk, Bible in hand, reading and watching.

He looked in the barbershop, smiling fondly as he recalled the many haircuts he received. He used to talk religion, politics and baseball with several of the barbers and found one that was as devout as he was. Often they would get together to read and discuss passages and stories. He knew that Sam Maxwell became a Presbyterian minister after the war. He had calls in several churches and retired from a large Presbyterian church in eastern

Pennsylvania. He also recalled hearing that Sam died when he was only sixty-seven.

The corridor where the gold had been stashed was going to be the last place he would visit below decks. He walked to the void, the lock was still in place, for he had relocked it after removing the gold, stashing the coins in his sea bag, wondering if it would be searched when they returned to their home port. He recalled being very nervous as the men left the ship after the war, but the SPs on the dock, just waved them through, knowing that these battle hardened veterans deserved to be treated with dignity, not suspicion.

After going topside, he took a few minutes to look over the plane that was bolted to the deck. He touched the propeller and ran his hand across the fuselage, feeling the rivets, recalling how the planes and ships of Task Force 58 destroyed the Japanese fleet.

He stepped in front of the ship's bell and tapped it. It was etched with the words U.S.S North Carolina and the date 1908. The old girl was in pretty good shape for a hundred and six.

Lastly, he walked to the exact spot where he hit Al Pederson with a pipe and then snapped his neck and tossed him into the churning water beside the ship. He kneeled down, folded his hands and prayed for God to have mercy on his soul. He cried for several minutes, the tears soaking the front of his shirt.

After he recovered he left the ship for the final time, turned and saluted again, seeing images of his former shipmates shaking their heads in shame for what he had done.

9

He drove to the hotel where he would stay the night and in the morning he would go to the post office and send Al's gold to Eleanor via registered mail. He still trusted the postal service to deliver the package worth nearly a half million dollars with no problem.

He checked in The Country Inn and Suites, opting for a whirlpool suite with a king size bed. After he tossed his overnight bag on the bed, he went to the main desk requesting a cab to take him to The Pilot House Restaurant, his favorite place to eat when in the city.

He returned to the hotel around 10, enjoyed twenty minutes in the whirlpool and then crawled into bed. He read for about a half hour and then turned off the lights and was asleep in minutes.

Saturday, June 21st, 2014

Southport, North Carolina
Wrightsville Beach, North Carolina
Wilmington, North Carolina

1

As soon as Rick stepped into his office, he saw the ghosts from the battleship. He found his way to his desk and sat down before acknowledging their presence.

He touched his braille watch; the time was now 8:14 AM. "You are all here early. To what do I owe the pleasure of your company?"

Justin Nonnemacher responded. "Al was camped out all night at a vacant house across from Larry Scott's house and I think as soon as his murderer returns from wherever he is, Al is going to kill him. I don't want to see his grandson paying for what Al plans to do."

Rick immediately phoned the Southport police and told them what he had just learned, without mentioning the ghosts.

The officer on the other end of the line asked, "How do you know this, Mr. Conlen?"

"I just received an anonymous call and that is what I was told."

"Do you know of any reason why someone would call you and not us?"

"No clue, but I feel that I have done my duty by informing you of this matter." He was becoming extremely agitated with the questions he was being asked, and had responded a little louder than he planned.

"Sir, there is no reason to raise your voice and I strongly suggest you don't do that again. I'll send a car out to see what is going on and if there is a vagrant on that property we'll soon know what he is doing there."

"My apologies. Thank you very much. Would you

please inform me after you get the person?"

"I don't think that will be necessary, Mr. Conlen. You have done your civic duty but unless there is any valid reason you need to know how we handle this situation, there will be no need to contact you." He hung up without saying goodbye.

Rick slammed the handset into the cradle, nearly breaking it. "How the hell could I tell him that a ghost told me about Brandon hiding out at that house?"

"Rick, we'll head over there and see what is going on. If he's booked we'll let you know and then the ball will be back in your hands as his lawyer. I'll tell Al to let them know this fact."

"I guess that's the best we can do right now. Hopefully the warrant will be issued this morning and Larry Scott will be brought in as well. We need to get to the bottom of all this, and soon, I think."

2

JoAnne and Eleanor were up early. They took showers, had a light breakfast of toast and coffee and were in the car and on the road by 8:30.

JoAnne kept trying Brandon's cell phone, but he either had it turned off or wasn't answering her calls. She kept leaving voice mails pleading with him to call her back, but they were wasted words at this point.

She turned toward Eleanor. "Gamma, I don't know how Brandon will respond to your being here, with Al inside his body, but I really think it is necessary that you see him."

Eleanor touched her wrist. "Dear, I understand perfectly. I certainly don't know what you expect, but to have the opportunity to talk to Al, even through Brandon, should be quite an experience. Not many wives have that opportunity at all and I don't want to miss the chance.

"I'm just excited that I'll see Brandon again. It's hard to

believe that all this has happened in less than twenty-four hours. I know in my heart that everything will be alright. We'll both get Brandon back and you'll have closure when Gramps's body is returned to Wilkes Barre. Chiyo hoped she'd be able to give me more information within the next several days."

"I am excited to get Al back, even just to bury his body. All those years of not knowing exactly what happened to him will be answered soon."

JoAnne was just ready to reply when her cell phone rang. "Excuse me. It's Rick Conlen. Maybe he has something new to tell me. She punched the green phone icon. "Hello, Rick. How are you?"

"I'm great JoAnne. There is a situation, though. Brandon is hiding at a vacant house across from Larry Scott's house, probably to kill him as soon as he gets home. One of the ghosts told me he was there and I called the police. They are sending a car out to hopefully arrest Brandon before he does anything and take him to the station. I'll let you know as soon as I find out anything more. Are you coming down today?"

"That's good news, if Brandon is arrested before he does anything." She patted Eleanor's arm after seeing the concern in her eyes. "Eleanor and I are actually on the way now and we should be there within the hour, if there are no traffic problems."

"Great. I hope Larry Scott comes home soon because the moment he arrives, he will be arrested and then I should get an opportunity to question him and Brandon. I know Larry's attorney and I'm going to call him as soon as Larry is in custody."

"I certainly hope that everything can be settled soon so we can all get back to our lives."

"Me too. Catch you later. I gotta run."

"Okay, Rick. See you soon."

Larry Scott was dressed and heading down to the desk to check out. He had a wonderful night's sleep, and another twenty minutes in the whirlpool bath this morning refreshed him. After checking out, he went into the dining room for a continental breakfast; a muffin, cereal and coffee was just what he needed. He finished eating, walked to his car and hopped in. He concluded his business at the post office and when he got back on the road again, he figured he'd be home by 10 or 10:15. He wanted to call Al's widow to tell her what he had done and inform her about the gold coins that should arrive at her house on Monday or Tuesday. He could only imagine the reactions of every postal worker handling that box. Would any of them take the chance of losing his or her job and face a long time in jail if they realized that there was almost a half million dollars inside. He really felt good inside knowing that he was going to get this all off his chest soon. He was certain he would not be in jail for any length of time because of his impending death, and he was hoping he would be able to wrap a few more things up in Southport.

Traffic was light and he figured he'd be home by 9:45, thirty-one minutes from now. He did have a little OCD when it came to scheduling.

He kept glancing at his side mirror and noticed an eighteen wheeler, nearly at the end of his range of vision. In front of the Mack were three compact cars, a minivan and a pickup truck with a cap. Everyone seemed to be driving the speed limit, and he quickly glanced at his speedometer. He was pushing seventy-five miles an hour. As he studied the vehicles behind him, he estimated that they were also traveling at roughly the same speed. The one exception was the tractor-trailer, which had swerved into the passing lane and was getting closer. He wanted to get away from the huge truck, but when he looked forward through the windshield he saw that there was no area he could pull off. When he glanced into his rearview mirror, he saw that the truck had picked up even more speed and was beginning to pass the other vehicles. Larry became a little concerned, the nerves of an old sailor, tingling, anticipating something to happen. He decided to pull out and pass the car in front of him because there was a lot of room in front of that car and Larry felt he might need that room. He just had a bad feeling growing in the pit of his stomach.

4

JoAnne and Eleanor were about four car lengths behind the big rig when it swerved into the passing lane. The back end of the flatbed trailer, piled high with long steel rods, nearly caught the front bumper of a very old car.

Eleanor saw that the car was a black 1932 Ford Roadster. She knew this because her dad had one exactly like that when she was a teenager. There were two people in the car; the driver had long white hair, tied back into a ponytail that was flying in the breeze. The passenger wore some type of baseball cap and as the trailer nearly took of the front bumper of the classic car, the blue cap was ripped off her head from the stream of air coming off the rear of the truck. She saw her reach up to try to grab it, but in a moment it was tumbling past JoAnne's car.

Since both of them were engrossed in what was going on in the outside lane, JoAnne didn't notice that she had pressed her foot down just a little harder on the gas pedal, increasing her speed by five miles per hour. As soon as she glanced at the car in front, she noticed the brake lights and when she applied her brakes, she looked in the rearview mirror. "Brace yourself, Gamma. We're going to get hit."

The only thing that saved Eleanor from getting injured too seriously was the air bag deployment.

5

After Larry Scott pulled out into the left lane, he shook his head; he realized that the speed of the truck was greater than his and unless the truck driver had extremely quick reflexes, his action was going to cause an accident, probably with more than two vehicles involved. He braced for impact and began to pray out loud.

6

Ernie Adams was anxious to get home to Southport. His son's fourth birthday party was scheduled for 2 o'clock and he had to get to the UPS store where the gifts he bought for Billy were being held.

For three days straight he had been driving long hours, dropping and picking up loads, making a lot of money. He became a long haul driver seven years ago after serving three years in the army, hauling supplies from place to place. He found he really loved this kind of work, but knew that he could earn a lot more in civilian life. He reached down to grab his coffee cup and it slipped out of his hand. When he attempted to retrieve it, he accidentally turned the steering wheel to the left, into the inside lane, never noticing the Roadster, nor the two vehicles that were about to collide behind him. He rescued the cup, having only spilled a little bit of coffee, and when he returned his focus to the road, saw he was in the other lane, heading for the guard rail, so he quickly pulled the wheel back to the right, overcorrecting, the trailer swaying. He turned the wheel to the left and then back to the right, finally straightening the vehicle. Then his phone rang.

7

Immediately after the crash, JoAnne felt some pain in her legs. The front seat had shifted forward a couple of inches after the impact. She looked over at Eleanor who seemed to be in a state of shock and then glanced into the rearview mirror. The hood of the car that hit them was standing straight up, blocking the windshield, so she couldn't see if the person or people in the car were okay or injured.

She pulled her cell phone from her purse, as she saw the driver from the car in front get out of the vehicle and start running back toward her car. She punched in 911 and told the operator what had happened. She was able to give her location from the Tomtom attached to the dashboard.

After she pressed end, the driver of the car knocked on her window.

JoAnne pressed the button to open the window and the man asked if she was okay.

"My legs hurt because the front seat shifted forward at impact, but otherwise I feel okay. Could you please go to the other side of the car and check my grandmother-in-law."

He hurried over and opened the door.

Eleanor felt a little groggy but when she felt a hand on her shoulder, shaking her, she moaned.

"Ma'am, how do you feel? Does anything hurt?" He inquired, looking to see if her legs may have been injured as well, but the impact only moved her side of the seat a little bit.

"I think I'm okay, young man." I don't feel any severe pain anywhere at the moment, but I'm sure this old body will be pretty sore for some time to come."

She turned toward JoAnne. "How are you doing?"

"Other than my legs I don't feel too bad. I am so glad you seem to be alright. An ambulance will probably be here soon." As she said this she looked in the rearview mirror and in the distance she saw flashing lights. Some kind of emergency vehicle was on its way.

8

When Ernie saw he was bearing down on the car in front of him, he tried to put on the brakes in time, but to no avail. He felt the impact and saw the back end of the car crumple as the weight of his vehicle, and the load he was carrying, push further and further into the car. As the car literally began to disintegrate, shards of metal, glass and fabric were blown backwards pelting his windshield, but not penetrating. He saw the hood of his Mack fly forward as hinges snapped, so he never saw the man being torn from the driver's seat, since he wasn't wearing a seatbelt: the body tumbled past his rig and banged into the guardrail.

The load of steel rods had broken loose, falling to the road, bouncing, turning and colliding with vehicles behind and beside the flatbed. One rod hit the street and cartwheeled, breaking the windshield of the Roadster, impaling the young woman to the backrest of her bucket seat. She only had a second to scream before she died. The driver saw what happened and threw up all over the dashboard. He would have nightmares for the rest of his life, never dating again, dying a lonely old man of 83.

Ernie finally stopped the truck and was elated to find that he suffered no injuries. He would be convicted of manslaughter and sentenced to twenty years in prison. Five years after his incarceration, he would be found dead, stabbed fifty-three times by an unknown number of inmates and guards.

Larry Scott felt himself being wrenched from the seat and as he plummeted through the air and then hit the guardrail, he felt no pain, just a calming peace. He assumed he was probably going to die from this accident   rather than suffer through the pain of the cancer that was eating away his body. After he bounced off the guardrail, his body spun under the flatbed trailer: miraculously none of the huge tires crushed him. He actually slid completely to the other side of the highway, hitting the bumper of a car that had already stopped. He saw the driver get out of his vehicle with a frantic look of fear on his face and rush toward his now still body. Fortunately unconsciousness overcame him and he would not awaken until later in the hospital.

10

One hundred feet above the scene, Alicia Nivens was recording the flow of traffic for a research project she was being paid very well to do. Moments before the accident, she had just turned the camera, managing to capture the unfolding drama below. She also had the presence of mind to call 911 and inform the police of the accident as it was happening. After shooting the entire crash area, she figured she would sell the footage to whatever news service was willing to pay for it and earn herself a little more income. She needed to come up with twenty grand quick to pay off a loan shark or she would soon no longer have the use of a leg, an arm, or more. after she told the loan shark she didn't have the cash. She didn't know if she'd get enough money for her video, but since there was probably a fatality, the man who was lifted from his car and bounced around creation, now lying still on the road, the value of the footage would probably increase.

She asked the pilot to hover so she could include the arrival of the police and ambulances. That would add a little more to the human suffering. She saw people getting out of their vehicles and zoomed in on them, capturing a number of visual emotions. She smiled and thought this was really good stuff.

Two weeks later, she would be in the same hospital bed that Larry Scott was going to be using in less than an hour.

Both of her legs and one arm would be broken and her face would look like it went through a meat grinder. It would be the internal injuries that would lead to her demise the next day.

Brandon hid behind the shrubbery when he saw the police car coming down the street. At that moment both he and Al had a strange feeling come over them. Feeling himself being pulled from Brandon's body, Al had no control over the situation and quickly found himself hovering over the scene of the accident. He was guided to Brandon's smashed car and saw Eleanor sitting in the passenger seat, just as the airbag began to deflate. He had missed her so much in his spirit state and now she was injured. He cried out in agony, and both Eleanor and JoAnne turned toward the most awful sound they had ever heard. Although neither woman saw him, Eleanor smiled and JoAnne immediately tried calling Brandon again. She figured that if Al was here, Brandon once again must have control of his body. His phone began ringing.

"Oh, JoAnne, I am so sorry for everything that has happened. Once Al took control I was only able to overcome his spirit one time. Are you okay?"

"Brandon, it's alright. You couldn't help anything that you have done. Eleanor is with me. We were in an accident on the way to Southport and…."

"You were in an accident. Oh my God, JoAnne! What happened? Are you and Gamma okay?" He interrupted.

"I don't think she's hurt too badly, except for being sore from the airbag deploying. My legs are injured because we were rear ended and the seat flew forward a couple of inches. I don't think anything is broken. The police and ambulances have arrived."

"What happened?"

She filled him in and then told her about the strong

feeling that Al was here looking at them right now. "We can't see him, but we heard a noise that sounded like pure agony. I just guessed that he might have left your body and that's why I called."

"I am behind some shrubbery in a yard. The home is vacant, so Al had me bring him here. His murderer, Larry Scott, lives across the street and I believe he came here to kill him. I think he believes that if he kills Scott, he will finally be able to leave the spirit world and move on to the afterlife. JoAnne there's a police car driving back and forth and looking toward where I'm hiding. What should I do?"

"Brandon, there is a lot going on that you don't know about. After we end this call, raise your hands and stand up to get their attention. When they arrest you tell them to call Richard Conlen. He's the attorney we met yesterday, if you remember. He understands what is going on and he will be able to help get you out of jail." She was hoping that Al would not return to Brandon's body, although she felt that that hope might not win out. Al still wanted vengeance and she didn't think anything was going to stop him from killing his murderer.

"Okay, honey. I'll do what you say and pray that we will all come through this experience. I'll talk to you soon." He ended the phone call, raised his hands and stood up.

12

Soon after the ambulances arrived, the two women were taken to New Hanover Regional Medical Center in Wilmington. After thorough check-ups, they were released. Luckily they were only bruised and though they would be sore for several days, the doctor saw no need to keep them overnight. She was totally amazed with Eleanor's resilience at her age.

After learning they would be released, JoAnne called a car rental agency and had a car delivered to the hospital. She was adamant that they would still get to Southport to see Brandon.

13

After Al looked in on Eleanor, missing her so very much and wanting to be able to touch her one more time, his ghostly senses picked up a sound that could even chill a specter. He heard a scream and knew it belonged to Larry Scott. His murderer was involved in this accident so he floated away from his wife and sought out the man who killed him

When he saw his old friend, Larry was lying on the street in front of a car. The car's driver was bent over him, looking him over.

Al saw that he was losing blood, had a broken leg and his right arm was bent back at an impossible angle. Most of his clothing was shredded and his right pant leg was torn off just below the crotch. Larry's face was cut and scraped at several places and some of his hair had been ripped from his scalp. He was twitching, but unconscious. Al could see him breathing and he wanted him to be live so he could kill him. He decided he would tag along in the ambulance since he really didn't need Brandon right now. He could possess his grandson at any time and would do so until he got the closure he needed and deserved

The ambulance arrived several minutes later and when the paramedics checked him they saw his medical bracelet. He was to be taken to the hospital in Southport where he had a large private suite. After the older paramedic, John Vargas, called his boss, he was authorized to take the patient to Southport.

When they loaded Larry into the ambulance, John said to his partner, "Randy, this guy must be a real bigwig for us getting the go ahead to take him to Southport. Guess I better step on it. He's not in any danger of dying, but he sure as hell is a mess. He's pretty damn old, too."

Patrolman Dan Zuminsky stopped the patrol car when he saw Brandon standing on the other side of the street with his hands raised. He was ordered not to harm the young man, just to arrest him and take him to the station.

Brandon fully cooperated; he was informed he was under arrest for trespassing, read his rights and searched. Zuminsky confiscated his phone, car keys and wallet, placing them in a plastic bag. Brandon was put in the back seat of the police car, but not handcuffed. He hoped this would all be straightened out soon because he wanted to get back to vacation with JoAnne.

On the way to the station, Brandon tried to remember everything that had taken place, but there were so many holes in his memory. When Al had taken control of him there were times that he couldn't even feel that he was himself at all anymore.

After he was booked, he was allowed to call Richard Conlen.

15

A cab pulled up in front of the police station and Rick Conlen stepped out. He opened his folding cane and after the cab driver placed his hand under Rick's elbow, they walked toward the front door. Once they were inside, the cabbie guided him to a seat and Rick sat down to wait for assistance.

A few moments later, a man sat beside him. "Mr. Conlen, my name is Sergeant Worman. I guess you are here to see Mr. Pederson?"

Rick shook his hand. "Yes, I am. I know he was picked up for trespassing, but may I assume you know the reason I wanted him detained."

"I do. It was a very strange request. I don't know if I fully believe in what I was told, but I've been informed that you are a trustful person and I'll be happy to release Mr. Pederson in your custody. He has been a model prisoner, for lack of a better term, since he arrived and I really hope his situation can be rectified. His wife must be going through pure hell."

"She is, and this morning she was slightly injured in an automobile accident just outside of Wilmington. She and her ninety-two year old grandmother-in-law will be on their way to Southport later today."

Sergeant Worman looked up to see Brandon walking toward them. "Mr. Conlen, Mr. Pederson has been released to you. I truly hope everything turns out well."

Rick stood up. "Brandon are you okay?"

"Yeah, Rick. I am. Thanks for getting me out.

Rick called for a cab and when it arrived, Brandon guided him to the car.

When they arrived back at Rick's office, they stepped inside.

Brandon sat down in a comfortable chair as Rick went to his desk and made a couple of calls. He reached JoAnne and handed Brandon the phone to talk to her and then he turned on the radio to listen to the news.

As the news was being read, Rick saw a couple of ghosts materialize in front of him. He had seen both of them before.

One ghost simply said, "Soon you will hear on the radio why we are here."

Brandon had finished his conversation with JoAnne and looked toward Rick. It seemed as though the lawyer was staring at something through sightless eyes and that freaked him out a little.

Rick turned up the volume and the DJ said, "Just a few minutes ago, we learned that Larry Scott has been admitted to the hospital. I was told that he was rear ended by a tractor trailer just outside of Wilmington and was transported here. He sustained serious injuries and is listed in guarded condition. We will update his condition as soon as we find out."

Rick and Brandon were in shock. Both wanted him to live so he could be questioned about Al's murder, and now he could possibly die.

"Rick what are we going to do?" Brandon asked.

"I don't know. I guess all we can do is wait and pray that he survives his injuries."

"He will survive long enough, Mr. Conlen." The ghost said.

"How do you know this? You are a spirit so how can you tell me he'll survive." Rick recognized the old man from outside The Pharmacy.

"Fourteen years ago, he ran us down with his car. It was entirely our fault because we were being chased by a couple of cops. We found a place to hide until they suspended the search. When it was dark, we worked ourselves out to the road and in our elation we were dancing in the street when Larry Scott drove over us.

"I knew we were both dead because I could see our broken bodies lying in pools of blood. He managed to lift our bodies and put us in his car and then he drove off. Later, he buried us in a vacant, wooded lot, a lot we found out that he owns. Our bodies were never found and we were listed as missing persons."

"My dad and I robbed a liquor store a couple of hours before we died." The woman said. "I can tell you where we had hidden five thousand dollars and we'd like you to make restitution."

Brandon said, "You two are the ghosts who tried to warn JoAnne and I about my grandfather."

They both nodded.

The old man said, "My name is Edgar Silliman and this is my daughter Nicole. You can Google us and find out about our crimes. Somehow spirits have the ability to know if someone in their past still living will soon die. There is no indication of Larry Scott dying. I think if he confesses to killing Al and to burying us, all three of us will be able to move on. We have faith in you counselor." He smiled.

"Well, do you know when I will be able to question him?"

"I think he should be conscious later tonight and by tomorrow he'll be strong enough for your interrogation."

"Thank you both. I will do my best to see that your bodies are found and returned to your family."

This said, the spirits disappeared.

16

The ambulance arrived at the hospital and the paramedics took Larry Scott to his suite. They were amazed with the amount of equipment in one single room and they looked at each other and shrugged.

Al stood beside the stretcher, watching a doctor check his vital signs. After he finished, one nurse drew blood and another took his blood pressure.

"He seems to be in pretty good shape for the trauma he has just gone through," the doctor said.

One of the nurses, Mary Spitzer, replied, "Yes, he is. I've known Mr. Scott for some time and he exercises regularly and for the most part he eats well and doesn't drink very much alcohol."

Doctor Morales listened to her intently. His grandfather was also in pretty good shape for his age, 87, and he knew that he needed to watch his diet a little better. Living to a ripe old age and enjoying the money he would save in his lifetime was a priority in his life, especially after losing his wife three years ago. His kids were married and his daughter blessed him with a grandson who would be seven in October.

After Larry was thoroughly examined, he was cleaned up, dressed in a hospital gown and put in his specially made hospital bed. He had never awakened, but about ten minutes after the staff left his room, his eyes fluttered open to see Al standing over him. He tried to scream, but nothing came out.

17

JoAnne and Eleanor returned to Wrightsville. They needed to change into clean clothing and get some food in their stomachs. Both of them were a little bit slower after the accident and surprisingly, JoAnne was in more discomfort than Eleanor. They walked into the room and both of them felt a chill in the air. If spirits were there, they would not show themselves.

"I don't know who you are, but if you mean us harm, we will fight you as best as we possibly can." JoAnne said, turning her head from side to side to see if the spirit or spirits were ready to be seen. No images appeared and in a few moments, the chill passed. Joanne breathed a sigh of relief because she had no idea how to battle a ghost, and she really didn't want to see if she could.

"Do you think we are alone, now, dear?" Eleanor inquired.

"Yes, Gamma. I think that whomever was here is now gone."

After they changed, JoAnne made a couple of sandwiches and Eleanor grabbed a couple of Cokes from the fridge. They took their late lunches down to the back porches and sat down to eat in silence.

JoAnne was mulling over what Brandon told her and that he would see her in the hospital tomorrow morning. He said that Rick wanted Scott to get a good night's sleep and around ten in the morning, a warrant for his arrest would be delivered to him in his bed.

They sat on the porch, quiet in their own thoughts after JoAnne told Eleanor her thoughts. By nine PM, both of them were ready for bed, although sleep would be a long time coming as they were lost in their thoughts of what had already transpired and what might happen tomorrow.

Sunday, June 22nd, 2014

Wrightsville Beach, North Carolina
Southport, North Carolina
Kashima, Japan (June 20th)

1

JoAnne awakened and looked at her watch. It was 7:39 AM and she wanted to get on the road no later than 9. She got out of bed, trying not to disturb Eleanor. She figured Gamma should get as much rejuvenating sleep as possible.

She turned on the coffee maker, having gotten it ready before going to bed. As it began to perk, she padded into the bathroom to take a quick shower. As she spent a few extra minutes just letting the hot water caress her body, her mind was extremely busy trying to process everything that had happened so far in, what, four days. Winning that money, seeing ghosts, having her husband possessed by the spirit of his grandfather and finding out who murdered him and suffering pain from an accident that could have been much worse. In a matter of a few hours, she would be reunited with Brandon and hopefully have Larry Scott admit to what he had done seventy years ago.

After she toweled off, she stepped back into the kitchen and saw that Eleanor was awake.

Eleanor smiled and when she sighed, she groaned a little from the achiness that ran throughout her body. She took a pretty good jolt when that airbag opened, but she was pleasantly surprised that she wasn't hurt badly. "Good morning, dear. How do you feel today?" she inquired.

"I'll live Gamma, but I think I'll be sore for some time to come. Would you like some coffee before you shower?"

She stood up and headed toward the kitchen, but she was wobbling and didn't trust herself to walk four steps. She sat back down on the bed and JoAnne handed her a cup of coffee. "Are you sure you want to go through with this today? You could stay here and take it easy. Steve and Mary said they'd keep an eye on you."

She took a few sips of the wonderful brew. "No, JoAnne. I really want to come along today. I know Al will be there and maybe I'll be able to see him one more time."

After she drank a half cup of coffee, Eleanor was ready to take a shower, but she felt she needed assistance from JoAnne.

When they were both dressed, JoAnne helped Eleanor to the car, although Gamma felt that she was much better and could walk on her own. JoAnne insisted that she help her and Eleanor finally acquiesced.

Moments later they were on the road.

2

Rick and Denise had arrived at the hospital at 9:15. He called Larry Scott's attorney last night and told him that the Southport Police Department was going to place him under arrest for murder at ten this morning. He explained the circumstances and that a witness provided details of what had happened on the battleship North Carolina seventy years ago. He didn't mention the paranormal aspect, but he was sure that the knowledge of him being able to see and communicate with spirits would certainly come to the forefront sometime during the interview with the accused after he was placed under arrest. Rick knew that the case would never go to trial because he was told of Larry's fast spreading cancer. The doctor thought that he would only have a couple of lucid days left and that Mr. Scott did not want to take any pain medication.

He was mulling over what he was going to say to Amanda Dotterel, when she arrived. He knew that she was very intelligent and was known in law circles as a real barracuda, chewing up the opposition in large bites with information she found out about their clients. She had been a lawyer for only seven years, but her win record was impressive. Forty-seven victories versus one loss. But this case was never going to trial, so Rick breathed a little easier.

Denise came to the table. She was carrying a tray with two cups of steaming coffee and a dozen doughnuts. She touched Rick's hand, not wanting to interrupt his train of thought and set the cup just to the left of his hand. She was learning a lot about the nuances of living with a blind person in just a couple of days.

"Thanks, Denise." Rick smiled. "I've thought out what I'm going to say to Miss Dotterel, but I think she will lose her well-known composure when she sees the ghosts from the ship."

"How will that be accomplished, Rick?"

"They all told me that if necessary, they would show themselves to her, but they would rather not. A lot is going to depend on how hard she fights to get Sanders' arrest dismissed. It could get a little hot in here, but I just felt that meeting at the hospital would be the best thing for our side."

"Don't look now, but here she comes." Denise looked at Rick, who was smiling. "Oops, sorry about that; forgot for a moment."

He nodded. "No problem. Does she intimidate you?"

Denise watched her walk toward their table. She was very tall, perhaps nearly six feet, with long, athletic legs and she could see her guns were sculpted pretty well too. She was pretty but on the plain side, with very little makeup and no lipstick. Her black hair fell down over the shoulders of a killer cream white business suit coat that was open revealing a bright red blouse. Her skirt was hemmed about three inches above her knees and she was wearing red high heel shoes. She was dressed to kill. "Good thing you can't see, Rick. She'd blow you away."

"That good looking, huh?"

"All that and a bag of chips. Time to stand up."

After introductions were made, Amanda and Rick sat

down, both agreeing to use first names. Denise walked away to get her a cup of coffee.

"Okay, Rick, let's get right to it; no dog and pony show. I have talked to the Police Captain and I will not allow this arrest to happen. My client is very ill and what good would it do for him to spend his last couple of weeks under house arrest in his suite here?"

Rick was ready to respond when he saw the ghosts from the ship standing behind Amanda, scowling.

"Man, you gotta make her understand what Larry did and how he got away with it for seventy years. He has to be punished, and if house arrest here is the best that can be done, do it, Rick," Justin said, and the others nodded."

"Rick what are you staring over my head for?" She turned around and saw nothing. When she turned back to him, his sightless gaze fell upon her.

"Nothing, Amanda. I just can't see letting him go, so to speak, without being under guard. He committed murder and he has to answer for it. Al Pederson's widow will be here shortly, along with her grandson and his wife. They are what this meeting is all about. "

3

JoAnne parked in a handicap spot because Eleanor brought her Pennsylvania handicap placard with her, in the event she would have to drive while down here.

They walked toward the entrance to the hospital and saw Brandon standing there, waiting for them.

He bounded down the steps and lifted JoAnne off her feet, spinning around twice as he passionately kissed her. He put her down and then kissed his grandmother. "Wow, it is so great seeing you both. I feel like I have been away for months. Having a spirit inside you really saps the energy. How are you both?"

"We're good, Brandon," JoAnne replied, although she wasn't quite comfortable being with her husband, not knowing if or when Al would possess him again. "We were banged up a little yesterday and Gamma is having some difficulty walking, but I think she's going to be okay."

He hooked his arm around Eleanor's and helped her up the steps. He could see she was getting a little winded and was moving slower than he ever saw her. At 92, she still could take care of her house and often times cut the grass herself with her riding mower. One day, a couple of years ago, he saw her on the second last rung of a ladder, cleaning out her gutters. He remembered just shaking his head, knowing that she would never allow someone else to do something she was still capable of doing. He did send in a cleaning service a couple of times to do the harder stuff, but Eleanor never liked having other people doing things in her house. She followed the cleaning team from room to room until they left. He kissed her cheek again. "Hope seeing Larry Scott isn't going to be too tough on you, Gamma. If you get upset and need to leave, just let me know. Okay?"

"Yes, Brandon. I will. I need to have closure though, especially since Al's body is going to be returned in the near future."

After Brandon gave her a quizzical look he turned to JoAnne. "What does she mean by that, honey?" He said in a whisper.

"No need to whisper," his grandmother replied in a harsh tone. "I still hear quite well and I am not imagining things. JoAnne told me. A Japanese diving team found an airplane they had been looking for. It had splashed down near the place Al was murdered and tossed overboard. The plane and your grandfather were encased in some kind of plastic like material and his body was preserved. They are bringing the plane and Al to the surface soon and then his body will be shipped home to us."

"That is amazing, Gamma. Not many family members can have that kind of closure. Their loved ones will be lost forever."

She took his arm again. "I know. When I saw the pictures of him in that state, so many memories came flooding back. If he can be removed from that plastic, I will be able to touch him one more time before we bury him."

He hugged her and then they walked through the doors, closely followed by Harmon Eckland and Lieutenant Marvin Greene of the Southport Police Department.

4

Chiyo and Yoshiro were watching the video feed intently. It was 8 PM, June 20th, 2014, in Kashima, Japan when Al Pederson's body, encased in the crystal-like substance, was loaded into a basket and being lifted from his watery grave. Soon it would be aboard the ship and after the plane was brought up and loaded, the ship would be heading back to port. Yoshiro was elated. Very soon, he would be able to place his grandfather's plane on display at the museum and his grandfather would receive a proper burial.

He was sitting right by Chiyo's side, squeezing her hand. Mesmerized, he watched the basket begin to head to the surface. The camera then pulled back to the work going on to free the plane from the ship. He saw the laser beam begin to cut through the crystal at a rapid rate. There were three men working to free the aircraft and he figured the plane would be freed in less than a half an hour. The plane was already resting inside four slings, ready to be pulled up as soon as the ship was contacted.

"Yashiro, this is so exciting. You must be so thrilled to see all the work being done to get your grandfather and his plane back to Japan." She touched his face, wanting him badly at this moment, but she knew he would not take his eyes off the monitor until the cameras stopped filming.

"Hai, Chiyo. My life's dream is going to come to fruition soon, and I am so glad you were here to be able to share my joy. After we can no longer see what is going on, I have something I want to tell you."

She nodded, wondering if he was going to ask her to marry him. As they continued to watch the unfolding drama so far away under many fathoms of water, she began to fantasize about her future as Mrs. Yoshiro Nagata.

5

The foursome strolled toward the cafeteria and when they arrived at the table, introductions were made all around.

Amanda immediately badgered Lieutenant Greene about his arrest warrant. "You have no right to arrest my client on the word of this man," she said, pointing to Harmon. "Something that may or may have not occurred seventy years ago demands more research than one person's word."

That being said, the ghosts from the ship decided to reveal themselves, creating a mild panic from the half dozen people watching the action from a distance. They had overheard Amanda's rather loud demand and it drew their attention toward her. Plus when they saw a police officer, their curiosity was piqued. One young man, upon seeing a policeman, decided he didn't want to stick around and he headed out the door.

Lieutenant Greene saw the man and immediately called the officer standing in front of the hospital. He knew the face and was pretty sure he was wanted for a crime, but he would leave that to Patrolwoman Laura Beck to sort out.

Amanda and Eleanor, never having seen spirits before, stood there with their mouths agape.

One ghost floated toward Amanda and said, "Ma'am, my name is LeRoy Hamilton, although I was known as Pops. My friends and I served on the North Carolina when Larry Scott murdered Al Pederson and stole over seven thousand dollars in gold coins from him. I don't know if the testimony of a ghost is admissible, but I strongly suggest you allow Lieutenant Greene to do his duty."

Her face had turned a sickly shade of gray, but she recovered quickly. In her short life, she had known people who had seen spirits, and she never ridiculed them, but she hardly thought she would ever see one herself, and now five dead sailors were in her presence. "I don't think the testimony of a ghost is admissible, but I think I have no recourse but to withdraw my demand." She looked toward Lieutenant Greene. "You may serve your arrest warrant, but I would like to be in his presence when you do so."

"Thank you, ma'am. Your demand *was* going to be dismissed, and I believe these spirits will accompany us to Mr. Scott's room. I would also like the rest of the people at this table to join us as well. This is an unusual situation that calls for unusual measures." He looked at his watch and said, "We'll be heading up in a couple of minutes, in case anyone needs to go to the bathroom, or get another cup of coffee." He looked toward the table. "Looks like doughnuts have been provided as well, so help yourselves. I'm going to step outside for a moment.

6

Patrolwoman Beck stepped behind a shrub beside the pavement outside the hospital. She crouched down just a little so she could see who was going to come through the door, and not be seen herself.

A moment later, the electric doors slid open and he stepped outside.

She immediately recognized him, even with the beard he had grown. When he was beside the shrub, she stepped out and grabbed his arm. "Hello, Sweet Thing. Nice of you to pay a visit to our beautiful town." She pushed him toward the patrol car and as she read him his rights, she frisked him, finding a pocket knife and brass knuckles. "Going to a party were we, Jimmy?"

"I didn't do nothing, lady. What are you rousting me for?"

After she cuffed him, she roughly turned him to face her. "Jimmy, Jimmy, there is no way I would ever forget your face. You sold bad coke to a friend of mine and he died in my arms. He was throwing up and gagging in his own vomit, you scumbag, and you're going to pay."

"Good work, Laura," Lieutenant Greene said when he arrived at the car. He looked at the prisoner and smiled. "Jimmy 'Sweet Thing' Reardon. Don't know why you came back to Southport, but it's going to cost you big time."

He dropped his eyes. "My friend Billy is in the hospital and I had just come down for a cup of coffee. I saw you and managed to hide my face behind a newspaper, but when I saw those ghosts, that weirded me out, man."

"Lucky us, Sweet Thing," Laura said. "Don't know what you are jabbering about ghosts for, though." She looked toward her boss, who nodded. "Really!" She exclaimed.

"Really. I'll tell you all about it later. Get his ass down to the station and process him in. It's a good day's work when you can get a piece of trash like him off the street before anyone else dies. I gotta head back inside and I'll probably be back at the office before lunch."

"Okay, Boss. I can't wait to hear what you're gonna tell me."

He turned on his heel and went back inside the hospital.

7

At 10:15, Lieutenant Greene knocked on the door of Larry Scott's suite. A nurse opened up and the entourage, including the still visible ghosts, stepped inside. The nurse fainted and the doctor examining Larry stopped what he was doing and quickly came to her aid, ignoring the specters.

Lieutenant Greene stood beside the bed and looked into the patient's eyes. "Larry Scott, you are under arrest for the murder of Al Pederson on board the battleship North Carolina, on June 20th, 1944." He read him his rights and said, "Your attorney is present if you wish to make a statement at this time."

Larry looked at everyone in the room, smiling when he saw his fellow sailors, knowing full well that they were dead. He nodded at them, not expecting any response, yet they all nodded back, but there was such a sadness in their eyes. He motioned for them to come closer.

"Fellows, I am so sorry for what I have done and God will see to my punishment once I join you all. I am also sad that you had to walk the earth since your deaths because of our connection when we were all alive. Please forgive me."

The ghosts turned their backs on him, signifying that there would be no forgiveness offered on this day; perhaps another time, if there was more time. He didn't need to know that their connection with him probably had nothing to do with them walking in the afterdeath.

He looked at Al's family. Eleanor had tears in her eyes, but Brandon and JoAnne showed absolutely no emotion. He said, "Mrs. Pederson would you come closer please?"

Although hesitant for a few moments, she wanted to get closer to him, wishing she had a gun, or the strength to end her husband's killer's life. "Why did you do this Mr. Scott? My husband was a good man and he never did harm to anyone. Yet you played God and killed him."

Amanda was ready to protest, but decided to hold back. She actually wanted to hear what her client had to say.

Rick wanted to hear if he would actually confess, and he felt Denise firmly grasp his arm.

"Mrs. Pederson. Over the time I knew Al, I knew him as a cheater at cards, a hard drinker and a person that did not share my values, although he thought we were friends."

Brandon started toward him, fists clenched, rage etched on his face, but he was stopped in his tracks by Lieutenant Greene. His hands were shaking and his voice broke as he said in a high pitched voice, "How dare you slander the memory of my grandfather. You're a fucking murderer and you have the audacity to smear him in front of his wife and me and my wife. If I could do it, I would end your miserable life right here and now." He was shaking so much and Scott showed absolutely no remorse.

"I am not slandering him. I am merely stating fact. A few of these ghosts, if not all, will attest to the fact that they always thought Al was cheating. Nobody could be as lucky as he was, winning nearly every hand. I don't even know how much more money he won from other sailors on the ship, but I assume he bilked them as well."

Eleanor began pounding him with the sides of her closed fists, crying in agony. She didn't cause him much pain, but it felt so good hitting him with all the strength she had. "You bastard. My husband would never cheat anyone. How can you even make accusations like this?" Lieutenant Greene gently pulled her away and she held him, sobbing on his uniform shirt.

Jeff Ambrose cried out sending a chill through every living soul in the room. "He was a cheat. I can't see any way that anyone could have that much luck. That's why I planned to kill him and take his money, too." After he admitted this, he started to vanish in ghostly flames, screaming as though in great pain. The sound lingered even as he vanished.

The living gasped at the sight and the other spirits feared that they would suffer the same fate as their shipmate. All of them had thought about getting rid of Al one time or another.

After everyone regained their composure, Larry Scott continued. "I knew where Al had hidden the coins and that night after a long day of watching for Jap planes and ships to return, my nerves were tingling. I had been praying, hoping that God would give me a sign. Receiving none, I still knew I had to take matters in my own hands. His eyes showed no remorse at all. May I have some water please?"

A nurse brought him some fresh water and he took a couple of sips. Then he coughed up some blood. "I don't think I am going to last too much longer, so I better tell the rest of the story. It was a very hot night and I heard Al get up and head topside. I knew where he liked to go when he wanted some alone time, and I also knew that nobody would be anywhere within hearing range. I decided to confront him about his cheating his fellow sailors out of their hard earned pay."

He took another sip of water. "I came up behind him, carrying a length of pipe. We talked for a bit and when I saw a shooting star, I took that as my sign from God. I told him I had to end his life. He was stunned and said 'You? I thought it would be Jeff or Pops. Why you, Larry? I never did anything to you.'

"'Taking money from my shipmates angered me very much, Al. You need to pay for stealing all that money; money that they could have used to feed their families, give to their churches, or help other people.' I told him. Then he laughed in my face and I raised the pipe and hit him on the side of the head. He shook it off, so I dropped the pipe and grabbed his neck, snapping it. I decided to lift him up and toss him overboard. He was still alive and tried to grab hold of the railing, but he was too weak. I watched his body hit the water, and I threw up."

As he spoke, he didn't look at anyone, he stared at a spot on the floor. When he finished he looked up, seeing anger and hate etched on everyone's faces, but he raised his hand palm forward, taking another drink of water. He coughed more blood up and the doctor approached him. "No, doctor. I need to finish this before I die."

In a corner of the room, a shape was forming. Eleanor

loudly whispered, "Al!"

"I've been listening to the bullshit being spewed by this man. A man who stole my money and came home, becoming wealthy and a pillar of his community. I never cheated any of my fellow sailors. I say this with God as my witness and if I am lying, let me suffer the same fate as Jeff."

The room grew suddenly quiet and was filled with a warm, bright light. Moments later, the light disappeared, and the remaining ghosts, with the exception of Al disappeared. The spirit of Pops dissipated through the floor, but Justin, Carl and Jim rose. They were smiling, even though they had committed crimes on earth.

Larry Scott began to sob and reached out to the ghost of Al Pederson. "Oh, Al. I am so sorry. I really didn't know that you were just fortunate, but what were you going to do with all that money?'

"I was going to give most of it to our church, and the rest I was going to invest for my family's future and now they have nothing."

Larry smiled. "That isn't true, Al. Yesterday I went to Wilmington and sent all the coins to your wife in a registered package. The coins are valued at nearly a half a million dollars now and she can do whatever she wants with it. When I came home, I knew I couldn't use money that I thought was tainted, so I put it all in a safe deposit box here in town. All the money I earned was through legal means and I used most of it wisely.

"I know you all hate me, and I imagine I will pay for my sins and discretions once I pass, but I hope the money can be put to good use." He coughed several times and then breathed his last.

Al floated over to his wife. "I have to go now, honey. I've always loved you and hoped I would be able to see you one more time."

He turned to his grandson. "Brandon, I am so sorry for what I did to you and JoAnne, but seventy years of being

136

in limbo, my body many fathoms below the sea, compelled me to take over your body. You are a good man and I wish I would have met you when you were growing up. Once I am taken from here, I will find your father and tell him what a good person you are." His ghostly smile was disturbing.

I guess my time here is up, and I wish you all good and happy lives." Having said this, he rose and then he was gone.

Friday, July 4th, 2014

Kingston, Pennsylvania

1

The Pederson family, along with Mr. and Mrs. Yoshiro Nagata, were seated behind a podium in front of the Pennsylvania National Guard Military Museum in Kingston, Pa., watching the parade pass by.

Two days ago, the Nagata's flew into Wilkes Barre in their private jet, carrying the body of Al Pederson, who was going to be buried on Independence Day.

Mr. Nagata had been communicating with the Pederson family ever since Al's body had been found encased in the crystal like substance.

Once his body and Yoshiro's grandfather's plane, containing the body of his grandfather, perfectly preserved were brought back to Japan, fifteen brilliant men attempted to remove the airplane from the casing. Al's body had been cut free from the plane, and as the men were slowly separating man and machine, the crystal began to reform, resealing the airplane again.

Over many time consuming days, numerous attempts were made to cut through the substance, but to no avail. One of the scientists involved in the project came to realize that they needed to place the plane back in salt water in order to complete the process.

Thousands of gallons of sea water was transferred into a tank. The plane was lowered in the tank, followed by technicians wearing breathing apparatus's

The removal of the crystal substance took several days but finally the plane was freed. Unfortunately, when it was removed from the tank, it quickly disintegrated. Plane and pilot were gone.

Nagata did not want this to happen to the body of Al Pederson, so he left it encased and contacted the family, learning about the parade that was being planned. He offered to fly Al's body back and attend the ceremony along with his wife of two weeks, the former Chiyo Nagana.

2

After the parade ended, Retired Admiral Anderson Worton, son of Al's commander, spoke, often looking toward the draped body of Al Pederson.

When he concluded his remarks, Eleanor Pederson stepped up to the podium, to thunderous applause. Her story was told and retold on all the news services nationwide and she was basking in the wonderful comments from friends and military personnel.

She waited for the crowd to quiet. The number of people that came to see her husband and to hear her words was nearly overwhelming. She brushed a tear from her eye and scanned the front row. She saw Steve and Mary Wright, Rick Conlen and Denise Scott. Even Larry Scott's lawyer, Amanda Dotterel had come. Looking off to each side and back toward the street she saw news trucks and vans from every service imaginable. CNN, FOX. NBC, CBS and the local TV channel WBRE was there. In front of her was a bank of fifteen microphones. She waved and then stretched a palm upward hoping to silence the throng.

"Congresswoman Sabilia, Mayors Taledge, Vonn, and Roberts, dignitaries and friends." She turned her head toward the people sitting behind her. "Admiral Worton, Brandon and JoAnne and Mr. and Mrs. Nagata, thank you all for this wonderful ceremony. It does this old heart good to know that so many people wanted to come out to pay tribute to my husband." She looked toward the shroud covering his body. "Al was taken from me over seventy years ago, not by the war he was fighting, but by a man he thought was his friend. Larry Scott explained his actions to me and my family shortly before he died and although I can never forget what he did, robbing me of my husband, I am a Christian and a forgiving person. I'm sure he is somewhere where people like him finally go after death." She shrugged her shoulders. "I believe that God determines the punishment that people like him deserve, but I guess I will never know for sure.

"My husband was a good card player, winning many, many more times than he lost and the gold coins that Larry Scott took from him, he gave back to me. I have cashed them in and received three hundred and sixty one thousand dollars after taxes. I've decided that most of that money should be used by veterans for veterans. I've written a check for two hundred and twenty thousand dollars for The Wounded Warrior Project, because the men and women coming home from the wars we're involved in sorely need the help of every American who lives free because of their sacrifices.

The rest of the money is going to my grandson and his wife to make their lives a little more comfortable. I still plan to stay in my home until I can no longer take care of myself." She giggled and added, "This old broad can still take care of herself."

The audience roared and applauded her for a full three minutes before silence was restored.

"I am glad that Mr. Nagata's team did not try to release Al from the substance he is encased in because when he freed his grandfather's airplane and removed it from the salt water container, the plane and his grandfather disintegrated. As most of you know he sent a team of divers back to the ship and they brought the remainder of the containers carrying the chemical that my husband's body is wrapped in and destroyed them. No good would ever come from saving and trying to use that substance. My heart goes out to him and his family. You know he has only been married for two weeks!"

The audience applauded the Nagatas, who stood and

took bows.

"In conclusion, I just want to say that today I am the happiest woman on earth because I never thought I would ever get my husband's body back, but I did." She nodded to two sailors in full dress uniforms who pulled the covering off, revealing Al Pederson. "In less than an hour, Al will be committed to the ground in Forty Fort Cemetery next to his parents. Someday I will join them all but I'm not planning on it too soon. Thank you all again."

Those seated, rose and once again there was a thunderous applause.

Al Peterson was home

ABOUT THE AUTHOR

Larry Deibert has written five novels; 95 Bravo-published by www.writers-exchange in 2004, Requiem For A Vampire-published by Mundania Press in 2007, and Combat Boots dainty feet-Finding Love in Vietnam (a rewrite of 95 Bravo), published by www.lulu.com in 2009. The Christmas City Vampire was first published by Bradley Publishing in 2012 and then by the author at CreateSpace.com in 2013. The Other Side Of the Ridge was published by www.writers-exchange.com in 2013.

He is a Vietnam veteran and is the past president of the Lehigh Northampton Vietnam Veterans Memorial

He retired from the U.S. Postal Service in 2008 after working as a letter carrier for over 21 years.

Larry and his wife, Peggy, live in Hellertown, Pa., where he enjoys reading and writing. He has two grown children, Laura and Matthew.

In their spare time Larry and Peggy love to travel to the beaches on the East Coast. They have gone on two cruises and in 2003 had a dream trip to England and Scotland. In Scotland, Larry was thrilled to play golf at the St. Andrews complex.

Larry would love to hear from you. Visit Larry Deibert's Books on Facebook, or send your comments to larrydeibert@rcn.com.

28448371R00081

Made in the USA
Charleston, SC
12 April 2014